A STOLEN KISS

"What an arrogant beast you are."

Cedric laughed with pleasure. "And what a fiery minx you are."

Expecting another angry retort, Cedric was startled by the flare of horror that swept through Emma's eyes.

"No. No, I am not," she fiercely denied, almost as if she were terrified of his accusation.

Cedric arched his brows at her unlikely reaction. "What is the matter? I like fiery."

"I do not particularly care what you like. I am a very calm and reasonable person."

"If you say."

Clearly sensing his disbelief, she abruptly turned the conversation.

"What is you interest in Lady Hartshore's companion?"

"Lady Hartshore is my aunt."

Her eyes widened in startled disbelief. "You are Lord Hartshore?"

"Yes."

"Oh. I did not realize."

He offered her a wicked smile. "No, I daresay you did not, or else you would never have dared call me an arrogant beast."

She sucked in a sharp breath. "You should not have kissed me."

"Not that I refuse to apologize for it. It was far too delectable. Indeed, I can hardly wait to do so again. . . ."

Books by Debbie Raleigh

LORD CARLTON'S COURTSHIP

LORD MUMFORD'S MINX

A BRIDE FOR LORD CHALLMOND

A BRIDE FOR LORD WICKTON

A BRIDE FOR LORD BRASLEIGH

THE CHRISTMAS WISH

THE VALENTINE WISH

Published by Zebra Books

THE VALENTINE WISH

Debbie Raleigh

ZEBRA BOOKS
Kensington Publishing Corp.
http://www.kensington.com

ZEBRA BOOKS are published by

Kensington Publishing Corp.
850 Third Avenue
New York, NY 10022

All Kensington titles, imprints, and distributed lines are
available at special quantity discounts for bulk purchases for
sales promotion, premiums, fund-raising, educational or in-
stitutional use.

Special book excerpts or customized printings can also be
created to fit specific needs. For details, write or phone the
office of the Kensington Special Sales Manager: Kensington
Publishing Corp., 850 Third Avenue, New York, NY 10022.
Attn. Special Sales Department. Phone: 1-800-221-2647.

First Printing: January 2002
10 9 8 7 6 5 4 3 2 1

Printed in the United States of America

One

Had anyone been in the lonely Kent countryside, they could easily have warned the oncoming coach that while its spanking pace might have drawn admiration in London, it was ill suited for the upcoming curve. Indeed, only the veriest fool would attempt such a maneuver.

As it was, the coachman was blithely unaware of his danger as he urged his pair to an even greater pace and sang a merry ditty at the top of his lungs.

It was not until they were actually upon the curve that he did futilely attempt to slow his pace, and by then it was far too late to avert disaster.

A shrill scream pierced the air as the carriage swayed precariously and at last tumbled into the ditch. Inside the ill-fated carriage Miss Emma Cresswell struggled to her knees and rubbed her aching shoulder.

Blast and damnation. Had there ever been a more ghastly journey? she wondered.

She should have known when the coach had arrived in London a full two days early that it was an ill omen. But rather than heeding her unease, she had hastily gathered her belongings and kissed her tearful sisters, Sarah and Rachel, good-bye.

After all, what choice did she have in the matter?

The carriage was to take her to Kent so that she could assume her new duties as companion to Lady Hartshore.

And anything had to be better than her previous role as governess to the wretched Falwells.

Besides, a renegade voice had whispered in the back of her mind, she would at last be far from the Devilish Dandy.

Surely it would be better to face a dragon of a dowager than the scandal her father always managed to create?

In Kent she would be free of the ugly whispers that followed in her wake. There would be no finger-pointing and icy glares because her father happened to be the most notorious jewel thief in all of England. There would be no more nightmares such as those she had suffered when her father had been lodged in Newgate, awaiting the hangman's noose. Or the painful combination of guilt and relief when he had escaped mere moments before his execution.

But as she had rattled for hours over the bone-jarring roads and her slender form had chilled to that of an icicle in the frigid January air, she had become increasingly concerned that she had been far too hasty.

What did she know of Lady Hartshore?

It was her Man of Business who had conducted the interview and ultimately chosen her from among the candidates. For all she knew, Lady Hartshore might be a ghastly tartar who would treat her with the same callous cruelty as the Falwells. Or she might even be so feeble that she would demand constant nursing. Hardly an enviable future for the next several years.

And she would not even have the comfort of her sisters' visits to ease her loneliness.

Her tumbled thoughts were eventually halted as she realized the jolts and sways had begun to increase at an alarming rate. Even worse, the coachman had begun to belt out bawdy lyrics that brought a blush to her cheeks.

Clinging to her seat, she had just been on the verge

of demanding the coach be brought to a halt, when she had been so unceremoniously tipped into the ditch.

With a shiver Emma realized she could not simply remain in the carriage to freeze to death.

Blast it all, she should have remained in London, she thought as she awkwardly crawled out of the coach. At least no one there was attempting to break her neck.

A sharp breeze greeted her as she leaped onto the muddy lane. It whipped her hood from her head and tumbled her honey-gold curls around her pale countenance. With an impatient hand she brushed the strands from her emerald eyes and moved to where the coachman was propped against the wheel, seemingly indifferent to the fact he had nearly killed them both.

She glanced down, easily smelling the cloud of alcohol that hung around his reclined form.

Drunk.

She might have suspected, she seethed with a building fury. No coachman could be so gloriously inept without being thoroughly bosky. And now she was stuck in the midst of the muddy, damp, godforsaken countryside with a sodden servant.

"Wake up," she commanded in surprisingly shaky tones.

"Tomorrow," he slurred as his eyes slid shut. "Be right as a fiddle on the morrow."

"Oh, do wake up, you fool." Emma shivered as another gust tugged on her cape. "We shall freeze to death if we remain here."

The only response was a soft snore as the coachman sank into a drunken stupor.

Emma stomped her foot in frustration.

Now what?

The narrow lane was hardly a bustle of passing coaches. It might be hours before someone came along. And while the horses remained unharmed and patiently

standing before the overturned carriage, Emma swiftly
dismissed the notion of using one to ride to safety. At
best she was a wretched rider, and with no saddle or
habit she was more likely to end up back in the ditch
than at Mayford.

Clearly her only option was to walk in search of help.

Emma heaved a sigh as she returned to the carriage
to remove the blanket and retrieve her muff. The last
thing she desired was to trudge through the mud for
goodness knew how long, but there seemed few options.
At least if she were moving around, she would be warmer
than waiting beside the road.

Pausing long enough to drape the blanket over the
slumbering servant, Emma determinedly scanned the sky
for signs of smoke. There had to be a cottage nearby,
she silently reasoned, and a cottage would surely have a
fire burning on such a chill day.

At last determining that there was a large plume of
darkened gray against the brooding clouds, Emma
squared her shoulders and headed for the nearby woods.

With brisk steps she plunged through the muddy ditch
and up the small hill that was covered with brush. The
going was not terribly difficult, although she knew that
her gown and half-boots would be ruined beyond repair.

But as she reached the thick trees, her pace became
less brisk and she began glancing over her shoulder with
increasing regularity.

It was not that she was a coward, she assured herself,
clutching the cape close to her shivering form. But having spent her entire life in cities such as Brussels, Paris,
and London, it was decidedly unnerving to be surrounded by such profound silence. She would have far
preferred to have been dropped into the meanest neighborhood of London than this isolated middle of nowhere.

There might be anything hiding among the thickening

trees, she thought as she peered into the shadows. Smugglers, highwaymen . . . cows.

Holding her muff as if it might offer protection from an evil scoundrel or raging cow, she kept her gaze firmly trained on the encroaching shadows. It was only reasonable to be prepared for disaster, she thought, attempting to excuse her unusual bout of nerves. If her father had taught her nothing else, it was that a young maiden should always be on her guard. And that nothing was ever as it seemed to be.

Intent on scrutinizing every tree and shadow, Emma hurried forward. She was so intent that she failed to note the growing soggy ground. Perhaps not so surprising for a maiden more accustomed to cobbled roads than the treacherous bogs that could dot the countryside. It was not until she had stepped forward and plunged her leg knee-deep into the gummy mud that she realized the extent of her foolishness.

"Oh . . . bloody hell," she cried, exasperated beyond measure.

Hiking up her skirts, she glared down at her missing leg, damning drunken coachmen, lurking cows, and muddy quagmires to the devil.

How was she to get out of this mess? Not only was her leg firmly stuck, but the slightest attempt to free herself sent a sharp pain through her trapped ankle.

Gads, but she wanted nothing more than to sit down and have a good cry.

Chewing her bottom lip and blinking back her threatening tears, Emma attempted to thrust aside her self-pity. She could cry later. For now she had to keep a clear head. She could not remain stuck in the mud for the entire night.

"My, my. What have we here?" A dark, distinctly male voice abruptly shattered the silence. "Surely it is too late for you to be a Christmas present? And those legs could never belong to a poacher. Perhaps a wood nymph, if a rather muddy one?"

The sardonic musings had Emma's head spinning around to discover a dark-haired gentleman attired in a many-caped greatcoat and tall beaver hat standing atop a small knoll above her. With his legs spread to a wide stance and his arms folded across his chest, he appeared inordinately large to the trapped young maiden.

Hurriedly lowering her skirts, Emma pressed a hand to her heart.

"You startled me," she breathed.

"I can readily return the accusation," he drawled, moving forward to stand at the edge of the bog. "It is not often that I stumble across a maiden stuck in the mud."

As he approached, Emma could begin to make out his features in the encroaching dusk. A strong countenance, she decided, with the firmly hewn features that revealed an iron will. His brows were straight and as richly dark as the satin hair. The nose was perhaps too long and his mouth a trifle too wide, but that did not detract from the fact that he was astonishingly handsome.

Still, it was the eyes that captured her attention. Thickly lashed, they were a peculiar golden color with a rim of dark brown around them. They seemed to glow in the half-light with a peculiar intensity.

It was only when she realized that she was staring at the stranger like the veriest half-wit that she noted the unmistakable twitch of his lips.

"It was an accident," she informed him, stiffening in outrage as his laughter rang clearly through the woods.

"Well, I did not presume that you had deliberately lodged yourself in that quagmire."

Cold, tired, and wishing she were anywhere but in Kent, Emma felt a flare of exasperation.

Gads, had she not endured enough? The last thing she

needed was this gentleman openly laughing at her predicament.

"I am delighted you find this so vastly amusing."

"Vastly?" He pretended to consider the word. "Perhaps not vastly. But certainly moderately. Yes, yes. I find it moderately amusing."

Her lips tightened in an ominous manner. "Are you going to help me, or just stand there, grinning?"

Supremely unaffected by her sharp tone, he slowly crossed his arms over his chest.

"I have yet to decide."

"What?"

He peered ruefully down at his gleaming Hessians. "I did travel all the way to London to be fitted for these boots. It would be a remarkable pity to have them ruined."

Why, the puffed-up coxcomb, she fumed. To actually put the gloss of his boots over the safety of a young lady . . . well, she would be better off without him.

"Very well. I shall do it myself," she gritted out.

"Hold a moment," he said with a chuckle. "I was merely jesting. Are you always so grim?"

Emma glared at the strong countenance. Although he had been handsome upon first glance, his devilish smile seemed to illuminate the male features. It was a smile that enticed one to allow inhibitions to be tossed aside and join him in laughing at the world. She felt the most peculiar heat singe through her blood before she was silently chastising her foolishness.

"I will have you know that in the past two days I have been rushed from my home, battered for hours over what could only laughingly be claimed as roads, nearly killed by a drunken coachman, and now stuck in the blasted mud," she informed him stiffly. "You would be a bit grim yourself."

"Perhaps I would at that," he conceded as his smile

widened. "Now, let us see about rescuing you, my muddy damsel in distress." Courageously tossing aside concern for his boots, he stepped into the mud. "Hold on to my shoulders."

Emma did as he commanded, although not without some trepidation. She was not in the habit of standing so close to strange gentlemen, and it was decidedly unnerving to feel the ripple of hardened muscles beneath her hands. This was no effeminate dandy, she realized, but a man accustomed to physical activity. It did not help that he had removed his hat, and his silken hair tickled her cheek as he bent down to grasp her leg just below the knee.

It was far too intimate for her peace of mind, and it was almost a relief when a sharp pang distracted her awareness as he gave a firm tug of her leg.

"Oh."

He immediately glanced up, the golden eyes darkened with concern.

"Am I hurting you?"

"It is my ankle."

"You must have twisted it."

The heat and clean scent of his body swirled about her.

"Yes."

"Forgive me, but I must get you free," he said softly. He waited for her hesitant nod before he once again lowered his head and gave her leg a firm tug. She bit her lip as the pain stabbed through her body, and she determined to be brave. Then, without warning, there was a sucking noise and her leg was free. Unfortunately it all happened so swiftly that Emma was caught off guard. With a cry she fell backward, but with graceful speed the gentleman grasped her tumbling form and with a twist he ensured that he hit the cold ground while she landed safely atop him. Momentarily stunned, Emma could do no more than stare at the dark countenance so close to her own. The gentleman, however, was much quicker to recover, and that glorious smile curved his full lips. "Now, this is a delightful predicament."

A thoroughly ridiculous heat flooded her cheeks as his arms pressed her close to that hard frame.

"Please, let me go."

"Come now," he teased. "I've ruined not only my boots, but my coat as well. Surely I am deserving of some reward?"

Emma once again felt those renegade tingles flood her body. Tingles that she refused to acknowledge as anything more than anger at his audacity.

"I have very little money," she coldly informed him.

His ready chuckle rumbled through the silence. "Then I suppose I shall have to make do with this."

With slow, exquisite purpose, his hand slid up the curve of her back, at last tangling in her thick curls. Emma's lips parted in outrage at his daring. She had every intention of giving him a sharp set-down, when he abruptly pressed her head down to capture her lips in a searching kiss.

Although Emma's life with the Devilish Dandy had been far from respectable, it had not included trysts with young gentlemen. In fact, Emma had never possessed so much as a gentleman caller in her entire life. But for all that, she had convinced herself that she knew all there was about physical desire. It would be pleasant enough, she supposed, to be held in a man's arms. But the kissing had always seemed rather messy, and as for all that groping . . . well, it had made her shudder to even consider the notion.

Now, as their lips met, she was wholly unprepared for the searing heat that exploded in the pit of her stomach.

No, oh, no, she thought with a flare of panic. The man was shameless to take advantage of her in such a fashion. She should be terrified, not shivering in pleasure.

But there was no denying the waves of tingling excitement racing through her body, shocking her with its fierce intensity. This was not messy. It was sharp and poignant and utterly delightful.

The lips eased their demanding pressure, but only to move and blaze a trail of fire over her cheek and down the line of her jaw. Emma's heart halted, then burst back to life with a thundering speed.

She wanted to lift her head so that he could nuzzle the line of her neck. To press her body even closer and thrust her hand into the midnight satin of his hair . . .

A moan of panic was wrenched from her throat as she realized the direction of her thoughts.

What was happening to her?

She was no common tart to enjoy being kissed and fondled by every passing rake.

Good gads, she did not even know his name.

As if sensing her sudden horror at her behavior, the gentleman reluctantly allowed her to pull back, although he kept her firmly anchored around the waist.

With a sense of shock she glared down at the smoldering golden eyes.

"Why . . . why did you do that?"

Not surprisingly, he gave a husky laugh. "What an absurd question, my dear. Why does any gentleman kiss a beautiful young maiden?"

With a commanding effort Emma attempted to gather her shredded composure. A deucedly difficult task when perched atop a very firm, very male body.

"How do you know that I am a maiden?" she charged in shaky tones. "I might very well have a husband who will be eager to kill you in a duel."

"So bloodthirsty," he teased, thoroughly indifferent to the threat of being summarily hauled onto the field of honor. "I know that you are a maiden by the innocence that shines like a beacon of invitation in those amazing eyes."

She sucked in a sharp breath. "Then you are a scoundrel for having taken advantage of a defenseless lady on her own."

"Perhaps a bit of a scoundrel," he readily admitted.

Emma determinedly arched from his disturbingly wide chest. She simply could not think while pressed so intimately to his hard frame.

"Let me go."

"You would not like to linger a bit longer?" he mused. "The cold and mud are a small price to pay for the pleasure of such delectable lips."

"You must be as bosky as my coachman."

A rather mysterious smile curved his lips. "No, just appreciative of magic when it occurs."

Her eyes briefly closed as she struggled to scrub away the memory of his kiss. It had been a brief moment of insanity, she assured herself. A moment that would never occur again.

"I shall scream if you do not release me at this moment."

His gaze slowly lowered to her lips. "I fear that there would be no one to hear. Still, you have made your point. Such a pleasant activity should be saved for more comfortable surroundings."

With a show of reluctance the stranger loosened his hold and Emma was free to scramble awkwardly to her feet. In her haste, however, she had forgotten her tender ankle, and stepping upon it, she gave a sharp gasp.

"Oh."

In a smooth movement the gentleman had also risen, and before she knew what was occurring, he had bent down to sweep her off her feet.

"Here."

Emma's eyes widened in disbelief. Never in her life had a gentleman handled her in such a fashion. Which was no doubt why her heart was racing and her breath coming in short gasps.

"What are you doing?"

Moving forward with astonishing ease, he gazed blandly down at her outraged expression.

"You are injured and cold. Like any proper knight in shining armor, I am going to rescue you."

"I can walk," she bravely lied, willing to crawl if it would remove her from the heat and sheer male strength of his body.

"Do not be a goose."

Short of a humiliating struggle that she was bound to lose, there was nothing Emma could do to alter her situation.

"Where are you taking me?" she instead demanded.

The golden eyes once again smoldered with amusement.

"To my home, of course. There we shall be warm and comfortable enough to continue our delicious activities at length."

With a sense of anticipation Cedric Morelane, Earl of Hartshore, watched the emerald eyes glitter with a wary suspicion.

It was rather bad of him to tease her, he acknowledged. Any young female would be frightened to be at the mercy of a strange man. But he had discovered a delicious enjoyment in watching her battle between fear and awareness of the attraction that had sparked to life between them.

By Jove, but she was a beauty when she was not puckering her features into a sour expression, he acknowledged. And having her soft form in his arms was giving rise to all sorts of pleasurable sensations.

He had never dreamed when he had chosen to walk back from the village that he would encounter this delectable minx stuck in the mud. Or that his desire to tease the frown from her face would lead to a kiss that had shocked him with its blazing heat.

A most delightful surprise.

Clearly not as pleased by the encounter as himself, the maiden gave a kick of her feet.

"No, put me down."

Cedric only held her tighter. "You shall have us both back into the mud if you do not halt your wiggling."

"I do not care. I will not go to your home."

He smiled down at the pale features. "Be at ease, my wood nymph. My intentions include nothing more scandalous than seeing you warm and your ankle tended."

She gave a shake of her head, the honey-gold curls shimmering in the fading light.

"No, please, I wish only to go to Mayford."

Her pleading words caught Cedric off guard.

"Mayford? Why?"

"I am Miss Cresswell, Lady Hartshore's companion."

Although Cedric had of course wondered why a pretty young lady would be in such a remote location, he had never anticipated this.

"You?"

"Yes."

"Good God," he breathed.

Not surprisingly, that sour expression returned to her countenance. "What is that supposed to mean?"

"I had hoped for an older lady with a bit of sense, not a reckless child with a tendency for disaster," he replied truthfully, careful to skirt a fallen log.

Her lips thinned to a dangerous line. "I will have you know that I am utterly sensible and highly competent. It was not my fault that Lady Hartshore's coachman is fond of the bottle."

He could not halt his rueful chuckle. Although James was a good soul, he did possess a habit of imbibing when he should not. Lady Hartshore had been most careless in entrusting Miss Cresswell to his care.

"No, I suppose not. Still, you are very young."

"I am three and twenty," she stiffly informed him.

"Indeed? I should never have guessed you had reached such a great age."

Those magnificent eyes flashed again. "You are mocking me."

Cedric gave an inward shrug. Although he would have preferred a sensible old tartar for his aunt's companion, he could not truly complain. It was not as if Lady Hartshore were in genuine need of help. She merely had taken a maggot in her head at the necessity of hiring Miss Cresswell. And a staunch old maid would certainly never have provided him with such an intriguing distraction.

Shifting her to a more comfortable angle, he determined to take full advantage of their momentary interlude.

"Not at all. I was simply wondering how you had made it to the age of three and twenty without having been kissed before."

A revealing heat flooded her cheeks. "I . . . perhaps because most gentlemen are not in the habit of accosting unwilling maidens."

Cedric allowed the memory of those molten moments to rise to mind. Although he had indulged in flirtations and possessed an occasional mistress, he had been as startled as Miss Cresswell by the sweet intensity of his desire. And there had been no mistaking the momentary response that had trembled through her own slender body.

"Not wholly unwilling, I think," he murmured.

She stiffened in anger at his charge. "What an arrogant beast you are."

Cedric laughed with pleasure. "And what a fiery minx you are."

Expecting another angry retort, Cedric was startled by the flare of horror that swept through her eyes.

"No. No, I am not," she fiercely denied, almost as if she were terrified of his accusation.

Cedric arched his brows at her unlikely reaction. She was clearly disturbed by the thought of her spirited nature and eager to deny her perfectly natural response.

"What is the matter?" he demanded. "I like fiery."

Her face had paled to a near white. "I do not particularly care what you like. I am a very calm and reasonable person."

Cedric was immediately intrigued. Why the devil was she so insistent? He had experienced for himself the fire and passion that smoldered deep within her. Why pretend to be a staid, unassuming milksop? Did she presume such traits were necessary for a companion? Or was there something deeper troubling her?

"If you say."

Clearly sensing his disbelief, she abruptly turned the conversation.

"What is your interest in Lady Hartshore's companion?"

"Lady Hartshore is my aunt."

Her eyes widened in startled disbelief. "You are Lord Hartshore?"

"Yes."

"Oh." A tiny tongue reached out to wet her lips, and Cedric was forced to battle the urge to once again taste their sweetness. "I did not realize."

He offered her a wicked smile. "No, I daresay that

you did not, or else you would never have dared call me an arrogant beast."

She sucked in a sharp breath. "You should not have kissed me."

"Now that I refuse to apologize for. It was far too delectable. Indeed, I can hardly wait to do so again."

"My lord . . ."

"Here we are." He determinedly overrode her protests as he rounded the stables and a groom came hurrying forward. "Greenly, go fetch James from the carriage he has overturned and then send word to Lady Hartshore that I have her companion safely installed at Hartshore Park."

With a speculative glance at the maiden in his master's arms, the groom gave a sharp bow.

"At once, my lord."

Confident that his servant would do as he bid, Cedric continued across the courtyard and at last climbed the steps to his vast manor house. He had just reached the door, when it was pulled open by a uniformed butler.

"Ah, Winters, have Mrs. Freeman come to the library and tell her to bring a fresh pot of tea," he commanded as he swept through the foyer and up the wide staircase. He did not halt until they had passed the landing and he had entered the warmth of his library.

As he had expected, a large fire burned in the grate, casting an orange glow over the towering bookcases and comfortable furnishings.

Glancing down, he caught the maiden worriedly chewing her bottom lip.

"You see, warm and safe, just as I promised," he said softly.

"Please put me down."

"In a moment." He crossed the patterned carpet and carefully placed her on a mahogany sofa covered in pale yellow silk damask. Relieved of his delicate burden, he swiftly moved to the side bar to pour her a large shot of his finest brandy. Just as swiftly, he had returned to her side, and pressing the glass into her hand, he lowered his large frame onto the cushion. "Drink."

"No, I dislike brandy."

"It will bring a bit of warmth to your chilled body. Unless"—he deliberately lowered his gaze to her soft lips—"you prefer a more direct and delicious means of creating heat?"

Having no difficulty following the subtle reference to their kiss, she sharply raised the glass to her lips and downed the shot in one gulp.

"There," she gritted out, only to ruin her show of bravado by giving a gasping cough.

"Good girl." He chuckled, taking the glass and setting it aside.

"I should be on my way to Mayford," she at last managed to rasp.

"You will go nowhere until a doctor has seen to that ankle."

"Ridiculous. It is nothing more than twisted."

"We shall see."

Her gaze narrowed in an ominous fashion. "My lord . . ."

"I thought you were calm and reasonable?" he gently reminded her.

Her lips snapped together as she swallowed her fiery words.

"You are very aggravating."

"Actually, I am widely considered to be a most charming and gracious gentleman. Indeed, I am quite a favorite among the neighborhood."

She met his gaze squarely. "If you say."

Cedric gave a laugh as she deliberately threw his words back into his face. So the chit was intelligent as well as beautiful.

A most intoxicating combination.

"You know," he mused as he reached up to toy with an unruly curl. "I believe that I shall enjoy having a wood nymph in the neighborhood."

TWO

Nearly three hours later Emma discovered herself tucked in a pretty rose-and-ivory canopy bed as the doctor examined her ankle.

She was not at all certain how it had occurred.

One moment she had been battling against Lord Hartshore and the very queer sensations he created within her, and the next, a stout housekeeper had surged into the room to take firm command of the situation.

With dizzying speed Emma had been swept upstairs and plunged into a hot bath. A maid ruthlessly scrubbed her free of mud while the housekeeper searched her luggage that had miraculously been retrieved from the carriage to discover her heaviest nightgown. From there she was carried to the bed with grim orders to not so much as twitch a muscle.

It was all very disturbing for a young maiden who had always been in firm command of her life. She was the one who was efficient and capable. It was she who gave the orders. Even the Falwells, who had treated her with such scathing disrespect, had depended upon her to solve their endless problems.

It was therefore little wonder she found herself bemused and not in small measure aggravated to discover herself bullied and outmaneuvered at every turn.

Blast that drunken coachman, she seethed as she

glared around the pretty chamber with its French lacquer cabinet and mahogany trellis-back chairs. If not for him, she would be safely installed at Mayford. She would not be stuck in this bed as the doctor poked at her ankle. Indeed, she would never have become lodged in the mud. She would never have encountered Lord Hartshore. And certainly she would never have been kissed in a fashion that had shaken her to the very center of her being.

Oh, yes, that coachman had a great deal to answer for, she told herself. And she sincerely hoped that he awoke with a wretchedly thick head.

"Well, it is not broken," the doctor at last concluded, straightening to regard Emma with a chiding glance. Almost as if he suspected that it was her own foolishness that had caused her injury. "But it is twisted."

"Then I can get up?" she demanded with a flare of hope.

"Certainly not," he briskly denied. "Not until the swelling has gone down."

"But I must get to Mayford."

"Tomorrow, perhaps."

Emma shuddered. Spend the night beneath Lord Hartshore's roof? The mere thought was enough to make her stomach twist in knots.

She wanted to be far away from the disturbing gentleman. She had already made enough of a fool of herself for one day.

"Impossible," she burst out before she could halt the word.

"I believe I know what is best for my patients, Miss Cresswell."

"Yes, of course. It is just . . ."

"Lady Hartshore will be quite understanding." He firmly overrode her protest, clearly as effective as Lord Hartshore and his housekeeper in having his way. She could only presume that stubborn tenacity was a trait common to those in Kent. "Especially since it was her coachman who caused your current discomfort. Now, I must speak with Lord Hartshore."

Predictably, the man paid no heed to Emma's protest that she was perfectly capable of traveling to Mayford, and merely collected his bag and left the chamber without so much as a backward glance.

Frustrated beyond measure, Emma briefly considered rising from the bed and sneaking off to Mayford on her own. She was no silly chit that must be told what she could or could not do. And she could not deny a rather childish desire to outwit Lord Hartshore at his own game.

But the delightful scheme was swiftly dismissed. Not only was her ankle far too tender for another prolonged walk, she hadn't the least notion where Mayford might be located. It would be the height of folly to be blundering around in the cold night with nothing more than overweening pride to guide her. And, of course, she could not ask for help from the servants without arousing the suspicion of Lord Hartshore.

It appeared that she was well and truly trapped.

A burst of unease flared through her body at the realization before she sternly attempted to dismiss it. She was being absurd. Certainly Lord Hartshore was a rogue, and his kiss had been highly improper, but he had proven he was a gentleman. Not only by carrying her to his home, but ensuring a doctor was fetched to care for her ankle. Hardly the actions of a gentleman planning to force himself upon her. That he could have accomplished in the woods with no one the wiser.

The sensible thing would obviously be to accept her quandary with as much grace as possible. It was only one night. And whether she liked the notion or not, Lord Hartshore was the nephew of her employer. Only a nodcock would deliberately court his ill will.

But for all her sensible reasoning, that ball of unease refused to be banished.

Perhaps because she had never encountered anyone like Lord Hartshore, she was forced to concede. Oh, she had met any number of handsome gentlemen. Lord Chance, who was soon to marry her elder sister, was undoubtedly fine of form. And, of course, her younger sister, Rachel, was inevitably surrounded by a bevy of charming gentlemen. But none of them had ever managed to disrupt her rigid composure.

So why had she reacted with such force to his teasing? Before today she had always shrugged aside such nonsense. But for some reason, her aloof manner had been embarrassingly absent in the force of his irrepressible amusement. She had been impulsive, unreasonable, and, yes, fiery. All the qualities she had struggled her entire life to suppress. Qualities that were far too reminiscent of the Devilish Dandy.

And as for that kiss . . .

She unconsciously bit her lower lip in an effort to stem the renegade tingles that assaulted her whenever she thought of his bold caresses. No amount of reasoning could explain such unwelcome sensations. It was all quite vexing.

A faint sound from the corridor had her instinctively thrusting aside her unprofitable musings, and gathering the covers up to her chin, she prepared herself for the arrival of Lord Hartshore.

She had no doubt that he would be her visitor. The notion that it was utterly improper to visit a maiden in her bedchamber would not deter him. Indeed, he would no doubt think it a grand jest if she were to point out his wanton lack of conduct.

Determined to maintain her composure on this occasion, Emma calmly watched the door slide open and Lord Hartshore step into the room. Her stern determination, however, was swiftly undermined as her traitorous heart gave a distinct flop at the sight of his tall, leanly muscular frame.

During their time apart he had bathed and changed into a cinnamon coat and buff breeches. Suddenly he appeared every inch the lord of the manor with his lean face freshly shaved and his midnight hair gleaming in the flickering candlelight. Only the golden eyes with their lazy amusement remained unaltered.

With a casual ease he crossed to tower over the bed. She gave a tiny shiver as he openly surveyed her pale countenance and tumble of damp curls.

"I have been warned that you intend to be a difficult patient," he drawled, clearly having spoken with the doctor.

Emma felt a faint flare of impatience with the tale-bearing man. Traitor.

"Not difficult, my lord, merely determined to be on my way to Mayford."

"In such a hurry to leave?"

"I would not wish to be a burden."

His lips twitched as if he were well aware of her true reasons for wishing to flee.

"I assure you that you could never be a burden. Indeed, I have never been more pleased to have a houseguest."

Such perfectly polite words, and yet, that frisson of unease raced down her spine.

"Thank you, but I really would prefer to be with Lady Hartshore so that I can begin my duties."

"How very conscientious of you, my dear," he commended even as the golden eyes sparkled with amusement. "However, tomorrow will be soon enough to begin your position. For tonight you shall be my guest."

Short of dragging herself from the bed, it appeared that she had little choice, she thought darkly.

"That is very kind."

He chuckled at the stiffness of her tone, then audaciously moved to perch on the edge of the bed.

"Not at all. This will give us the perfect opportunity to become better acquainted. I must admit to being very curious about you."

Emma sucked in a sharp breath. Not only at his daring proximity, but at the mere mention of becoming better acquainted. Under the best of circumstances she would never encourage this gentleman. He was far too disturbing for her peace of mind. With the secrets she was determined to keep hidden, it would be utter ruin.

Still, she was wise enough to realize that any overt refusal to discuss herself was bound to create precisely the sort of suspicion she was hoping to avoid. Far better to give sway and hope his interest was as fleeting as most gentlemen's.

"What is it that you wish to know?"

He studied her deliberately bland countenance with a probing gaze.

"What made you chose to come to Kent?"

"I was in need of employment," she retorted simply.

Almost imperceptively, that disturbing gaze flicked to the large emerald that hung around her neck before returning to her countenance. Not for the first time Emma cursed the brilliant gem that had been given to her by her father. More than once she had considered giving it to a charity or simply tossing it in the rubbish. Certainly no mere companion would have need for such a stone.

But for reasons she never sought to pursue, the emerald remained around her neck. Now she wished she had at least kept it locked in her luggage.

Oddly, however, Lord Hartshore made no comment on the priceless fortune sparkling upon her bosom.

"According to my aunt, you were employed as a governess."

"Yes, but I desired a change."

"Surely there were opportunities for you in London?" he persisted.

"London no longer held appeal for me, my lord."

A rather speculative gleam entered his eyes. "A broken heart?"

Emma swallowed her tart reply. Why not allow him to believe such a ridiculous notion? It would at least keep him off the scent of her true reason for leaving London.

"Of a sort." She pretended to hedge.

"He must be a witless fool to have allowed you to slip from his grasp."

Her lips twisted at the thought of the Devilish Dandy.

"On the contrary, he is exceptionally clever."

"You know, you intrigue me greatly, Miss Cresswell," he murmured.

Emma clenched her hands beneath the cover. In three and twenty years she had never intrigued any gentleman. Why now? And why this man?

"I assure you there is nothing intriguing about me. I am a simple servant, nothing more."

Placing his hands on the mattress, he slowly leaned forward. "There is nothing simple about you, my little wood nymph."

Emma sank deeper into the pillows behind her. "I wish you would not call me that."

His low chuckle sent a rash of awareness over her skin.

"Why not? Such eyes could not belong to a mere mortal. And, of course, only a magical creature could have enchanted me with a mere kiss."

Her eyes widened as a shock of heat raced through her body. No, she chastised herself sternly. He was merely flirting. He no doubt flirted with every female to cross his path. She was being a dolt to shake and shiver at his practiced charm.

"My lord, this is highly improper," she protested in cold tones.

He shrugged his unconcern. "I have never been overly fond of propriety. Such a tiresome way to live one's life."

She did not need to pretend her expression of disapproval. He sounded remarkably like her father.

"I happen to believe that propriety and respectability are highly desirable traits."

The golden eyes narrowed at the edge in her tone. "Why? They speak nothing of a person's heart or the beauty of their soul. I am acquainted with many so-called respectable and proper individuals who are far too concerned with what others think rather than merely being concerned for others."

She was not to be swayed by pretty words.

"And I am acquainted with many rogues who believe that charm is a substitute for morals."

His brows rose at her accusation. "And you believe me to be a rogue?"

"Are you not?"

"No," he retorted in a husky voice. "Simply a gentleman bewitched by a wood nymph."

Drat. How did he always manage to tumble her off guard?

"Sir, you really must halt your foolishness," she commanded in less than even tones.

"Why?" Unbelievably, he lifted a hand to toy with a stray curl that lay upon her cheek. "You are determined to behave as if nothing out of the ordinary occurred."

Her heart raced out of control, but with determination she held on to her composure. She might react to this gentleman like a fool, but she did not have to behave as one.

"Of course it did. I was nearly killed by a drunken

coachman, my foot became lodged in the mud, and a strange gentleman forced himself upon me. Hardly an ordinary day for any lady."

Her stern chastisement did nothing more than deepen his amusement.

"You did not mention the magic that shimmered in the air when our lips met."

No, she would not recall that kiss, she told herself. It was a memory best buried and forgotten.

"I do not believe in magic."

"How wretchedly dismal." His finger boldly trailed over the heated skin of her cheek. "The world would be a dull place indeed without magic and ghosts and beautiful wood nymphs."

Calm and reasonable, she frantically reminded herself. Calm and reasonable. Calm and reasonable . . . a shudder raced through her body.

"You cannot believe in such nonsense?"

He gazed deep into her wide eyes. "With all my heart."

A brief, breathless moment passed between them.

Magic.

It was ludicrous. As ludicrous as ghosts and wood nymphs. And yet . . . what other explanation was there for the blaze of sensations that coursed through her body whenever he was near?

No, she was simply overly tired, she desperately told herself. And no doubt she was coming down with a chill.

Magic? Fah. More like a brain fever.

On the point of demanding that Lord Hartshore leave her in peace, she was saved the necessity as the stout housekeeper entered the room, carrying a large tray.

"Here we are, luv," she boomed as she crossed toward the bed. "A nice bowl of soup and bread fresh from the oven. Just what you need to warm you up a mite."

Forced to move by the advancing servant, Lord Hartshore rose reluctantly to his feet as Mrs. Freeman settled the tray over her patient's legs.

Silently Emma breathed a sigh of relief. Thank goodness for overbearing housekeepers.

"This is very kind, Mrs. Freeman," she murmured, her mouth already watering at the delicious aroma floating through the air.

"Mind you, eat every scrap."

"Yes, I will."

Satisfied that Emma was suitably cowed, the housekeeper turned her commanding attention in Lord Hartshore's direction.

"And you, sir, should not be in here," she informed him in stern tones.

That irrepressible amusement shimmered in his eyes. "I was just leaving."

She shook a finger in his direction. "See that you do."

"But of course."

She sent him a warning frown before turning and marching out of the room. With a laugh Lord Hartshore glanced down at Emma's pale face.

"I shall no doubt receive cold gruel for my dinner."

"It would serve you right," she promptly retorted. "I told you that it was not proper."

He gazed at her for a moment before giving a rueful shrug. "Very well, my prim and prickly Miss Cresswell. I will stop in later to see how you go on." Without warning he leaned down to place a gentle kiss on her forehead. Emma gasped and he pulled back to meet her startled gaze. "Magic."

At Lord Hartshore's request the carriage rumbled over the road to Mayford at a sedate pace. Although Miss Cresswell had sternly claimed her ankle was much improved, he had no desire to have it rattled over rough roads. Besides, after her rather spectacular ride the previous day, he was certain she would appreciate a more mundane means of travel.

Not that she appeared particularly appreciative, he wryly acknowledged.

Leaning back into his cushioned seat, he regarded the maiden across from him. Since she had awoken that morning, she treated him with a frosty composure that was meant to keep him at a distance. His every attempt at conversation was countered with an icy retort, and when he insisted upon helping her to the carriage, she was as rigid as a stick of wood.

He could not deny he found her stiff formality a source of amusement. She might desperately desire to appear a staid servant, but he was intimately familiar with the fire that smoldered just below the surface. And it was that knowledge that pricked Miss Cresswell like a thorn she could not dislodge.

His lips unconsciously curved into a smile. What an odd combination she was, he silently acknowledged. All prim and staunch on the outside and inside a muddle of innocent passion. And, of course, there was the mystery of her presence in Kent. She was no simple companion, of that he was sure. Her dress and clothing marked her a lady, while that emerald spoke of considerable wealth. Such maidens did not become companions unless they were fleeing from something.

But what?

He had already dismissed her insinuation it was a lover. No beautiful maiden could remain so deliciously innocent had she shown encouragement to a gentleman.

Perhaps it was an overbearing father, he mused, or a wicked stepmother. Or an unwanted marriage.

He gave a faint shrug. Whatever the mystery, he would eventually unravel it.

He was nothing if not persistent.

Stretching out his legs, Cedric allowed his gaze to drift over the purity of her profile.

"You are very quiet this morning," he at last murmured. "Are you quite certain that your ankle is not troubling you?"

With a deliberate show of reluctance, she turned from the window she had been regarding with rigid fascination.

"It is only a bit sore," she assured him in cool tones.

He tilted his head to one side. "Then perhaps you are anxious at the upcoming meeting with my aunt?"

For a moment he thought she might refuse to answer, then apparently realizing he was closely related to her employer and therefore in a position to be humored, her lips thinned.

"Of course I am," she conceded. "I was hired by her Man of Business. It might be that I shall not suit her needs."

Cedric laughed at the mere notion. His dear, rather addlepated aunt had already convinced herself that Miss Cresswell's presence was vital to Mayford. Nothing would sway her now.

"You need have no fears. My aunt is a kind soul with a generous heart. She will be delighted to have you in her home."

"You did not possess such faith in my abilities yesterday," she reminded him in dry tones.

"I will admit a measure of surprise at finding my aunt's companion to be such a young and lovely maiden. Thankfully I have reconciled myself with the knowledge that what you lack in age is more than compensated by your numerous other qualities."

The beautiful eyes flashed at his teasing, but her expression never altered.

"Lady Hartshore may find my other qualities not to her liking."

"She will adore you," he assured her. "Just as I have no doubt you will adore her."

There was another pause before she allowed herself to utter the question that had no doubt bothered her for days.

"What is she like?"

Cedric found himself hesitating. Although he was deeply devoted to his aunt Cassie, he was not indifferent to the knowledge most considered her distinctly odd.

"That is rather a difficult question," he conceded.

"Why?"

"Well, as I said, she is very kind. Indeed, there is not a tenant or family within the county that she has not helped in some way."

"She sounds lovely."

"She is."

The emerald eyes sharpened. "There is something that you are not telling me."

Cedric carefully considered his words. "She has a few . . . peculiar notions."

An air of wariness settled around her. "How peculiar?"

"They are harmless," he temporized, then, hoping to distract her, he pointed out the window. "Ah, there is Mayford."

With a suspicious glance she slowly turned to regard the large stone structure just coming into view. Thankfully the sprawling mansion appeared to wipe the questions tumbling on her delectable lips from her mind.

"Gracious," she breathed.

It was an impressive sight, Cedric conceded. Although not as large or ancient as Hartshore Park, the house was nicely situated with towering Ionic columns topped by statues of ancient Grecian gods. Carved into the smooth stones were delicate cameos of robed Greeks with heavy urns atop the roof. Four sweeping steps led to the double doors framed by large arched windows.

"My aunt's grandfather had it constructed for his new bride," he explained as they turned onto the tree-lined drive. "A rather whimsical fancy, but it suits my aunt and her brother."

"I did not realize it would be so vast."

"It is very comfortable."

She worried her bottom lip in a manner he was beginning to realize meant she was inwardly agitated.

"I shall no doubt spend most of my days lost."

Cedric felt a burst of sympathy for the young maiden. Whatever her reasons for coming to Kent, it could not be easy to be thrust among strangers.

"Nonsense," he said gently. "You shall soon feel quite at home."

"Yes," she said doubtfully.

The carriage pulled to a smooth halt, and without waiting for the groom to assist him, Cedric pushed open the door and vaulted onto the paved courtyard. Turning around he prepared to lift Miss Cresswell from her seat.

"Here we go."

"No." She sank back into the leather cushion with a stubborn expression. "I prefer to walk."

His lips twitched. She was a contrary wench, but he admired her courage.

"Very well, Miss Cresswell."

He waited for her to awkwardly climb down, then, firmly placing her hand upon his arm for support, he slowly led her up the steps.

With commendable speed the door was pulled open by a uniformed butler so Cedric could escort the limping maiden into the foyer.

"Welcome, my lord," the servant murmured with a bow.

"I come bearing gifts, Mallory," Cedric retorted.

The aged butler gave a faint smile. "So I see. Welcome to Mayford, Miss Cresswell."

"Thank you."

Mallory turned back to Cedric. "Lady Hartshore is in the front parlor."

"I will show myself in."

"Very good, sir."

With the same care he had shown earlier, Cedric led a silent Miss Cresswell up the staircase paneled in a rich mahogany. For a moment he considered warning the maiden of the upcoming confrontation. After all, his aunt and her elder brother were bound to be a shock. But a brief glance at her set features warned him that she was already battling a flare of nerves. He was certain that the confession of his relative's odd fancies would be her undoing.

Reaching the landing, he moved to push open the door to the front parlor, then escorted his companion into the long room. He watched her eyes widen as her gaze swept over the English rosewood furnishings and tapestries gracing the walls. A white marble chimneypiece and elegantly scrolled cornice completed the image of splendid elegance.

She was given little opportunity to appreciate her surroundings, however, as a tiny lady with a fluff of gray curls sprang to her feet and rushed across the carpet.

"Cedric, at last," Lady Hartshore chirped, her narrow features more birdlike than ever as she peered at her new companion.

"I have brought Miss Cresswell safe and sound, Aunt Cassie," he assured his fluttering relative.

"Thank goodness." She reached out to lay a hand upon Miss Cresswell's arm. "My dear, you have no notion how I have fretted. I am so wretchedly sorry. James promised me faithfully that he would not so much as have a sip. If I had suspected for a moment . . . well, it is too late to put the milk back into the jug once it has spilt, as my Fredrick would say."

Miss Cresswell blinked as the words tumbled from Lady Hartshore's lips at breathless speed, but accustomed to his aunt's habit of chattering without pause, Cedric merely chuckled.

"Aunt Cassie, I believe Miss Cresswell would be more comfortable seated."

"Oh, of course. Forgive me." Lady Hartshore fluttered behind Cedric as he escorted Miss Cresswell to a velvet-covered sofa. Then, neatly pushing him aside, she dropped herself on the cushion next to her guest. "Such a dreadful thing to have happened, my dear. I hope that it hasn't quite turned you against us."

"It was an accident," Miss Cresswell graciously conceded.

Lady Hartshore gave a click of her tongue. "I should have sent dear Cedric's coachman as he requested, but James did promise and I did not like him to think that I did not trust him. He has worked very hard, you see, to become a more dependable father and husband, and I always feel that we should do our best to support such worthy efforts. Are you in terrible pain?"

Covertly moving to stand beside the blazing fire, Cedric watched as Miss Cresswell attempted to follow his aunt's tumbled speech.

"Not at all," she bravely lied. "I hardly feel a twinge."

"She should remain off her feet for the next few days," Cedric interposed in firm tones.

Not surprisingly Miss Cresswell flashed him a glittering glance for his efforts, but his aunt was giving him a firm nod of her head.

"Of course."

"I assure you that I am quite well," the maiden perversely argued, clearly disliking his interference.

Lady Hartshore reached out to pat her hand. "Cedric

is quite right. You should rest until your ankle is fully healed."

"Lord Hartshore is very kind, but I believe I am capable of knowing what is best for my ankle."

The older matron gave a tinkling laugh. "Oh, no, Cedric is always right, I fear. It is really his most annoying fault."

Cedric tilted back his head to chuckle as the emerald gaze once again snapped in his direction.

"There you have it, my little wood nymph. I am always right," he drawled.

Three

Cedric watched in pleasure as a faint color crept beneath the pale features. How lovely she was when she forgot to pinch her expression into prim lines, he thought. As lovely as any maiden who graced the drawing rooms of London. It made him determined to wipe those tight lines away forever. No woman should spend her life all pinched and puckered.

"Wood nymph?" Lady Hartshore chirped in confusion.

Cedric kept his gaze trained on the narrowed emerald eyes. "I came upon her in the woods with her hair flying and those amazing eyes flashing. I thought she must be a nymph come to bewitch me."

Lady Hartshore clapped her hands. "How delightful. She does rather look like a sprite. Although she is very pale." Her head tilted to an inquisitive angle. "Was it a ghastly journey?"

With a warning frown at the gentleman leaning nonchalantly against the mantel, Miss Cresswell returned her attention to her employer.

"Fairly ghastly."

Lady Hartshore heaved a sympathetic sigh. "I do hate to travel. All that swaying and bumping. And it invariably rains as if God is punishing one for not staying home, where one belongs. Of course, if you are like most young people these days, you prefer to be forever gadding around from one place to another."

"Oh, no, I prefer to live quietly," Miss Cresswell insisted in sincere tones.

"Then we shall suit each other perfectly."

"Yes." Miss Cresswell conjured a hesitant smile. "Although I am not quite certain what my duties shall be."

"Well, to be honest, I haven't the faintest notion. What does a companion usually do?"

Cedric watched Miss Cresswell blink in surprise. "Well . . . I suppose they answer correspondence and read aloud and ensure that their employer is always comfortable."

Lady Hartshore took a moment to ponder the suggestions.

"That seems rather dull for you, my dear," the older woman at last concluded. "A lovely young maiden should be enjoying the local entertainments, not dancing attendance upon an old woman."

Cedric lifted a hand to cover his twitching lips as he prepared for the revelations to come. The prim and proper Miss Cresswell was about to discover the true reason his aunt had hired a companion.

"I do not understand." Miss Cresswell's brows puckered. "I am here to be your companion, am I not?"

"Certainly," Lady Hartshore assured her with another pat on the hand. "Fredrick was quite emphatic that I must hire a companion."

"Fredrick?"

"My dear husband."

"Oh . . . but . . . I presumed you were a widow."

Cedric's hidden smile widened. He was far too familiar with his aunt to consider the notion she might remain discreet. She found nothing odd at all in her unusual notions.

"I am. Fredrick died several years ago," Lady Hartshore said serenely. "Still, he visits me quite frequently. I should be lost without him, you know."

The slender frame slowly stiffened as Miss Cresswell struggled to accept the truth of Lady Hartshore's words.

"Fredrick is a . . . ghost?"

As always, Lady Hartshore misinterpreted the hint of horror that accompanied her blithe confession.

"Oh, you needn't fear," she assured the younger woman. "He isn't a frightening specter. He merely bears me company and makes suggestions from time to time."

"I see."

"I must admit I was quite astonished when he first told me to hire a companion," Lady Hartshore continued to chatter, blissfully unaware of the rather sick expression on her guest's countenance. "After all, I am not feeble in any way. But I have learned to always heed dear Fredrick's suggestions. You know, he once awoke me and told me to go down to the parlor and I discovered that a candle had caught the drapes on fire. And then there was the morning he locked Bart in his chambers so that he could not go in search of his treasure and we had that terrible flood. Of course, Bart was quite furious, and to be perfectly honest I am not certain that he has completely forgiven Fredrick. Still, it has taught me to always mind what Fredrick tells me."

Miss Cresswell's lips opened once, twice, and then three times before she could speak.

"Are you telling me that you hired me because a ghost told you to?"

"Oh, no," the countess denied, her expression sweetly sincere. "It was Fredrick who suggested that I hire a companion, but it was Mrs. Borelli who actually read the tea leaves and determined that you were the perfect choice."

Cedric felt a mixture of amusement and sympathy as Miss Cresswell's hand dropped to clench in her lap. Even those closely acquainted with his aunt were at times disarmed by her casual reference to her dead husband. And, of course, it did not improve matters that her cook was a proclaimed fortune-teller. All very disturbing for a maiden who valued respectability above all things.

"Oh," she muttered.

"And now that you have arrived, I am quite certain the tea leaves were right. What a delight it will be to have a young person in the house. Bart and I have become quite tedious with only the two of us to bear each other company."

Miss Cresswell was shaking her head before Lady Hartshore even finished.

"Actually . . . I mean . . . perhaps . . ." The maiden stammered in an attempt to extricate herself from the clearly disturbing encounter.

Cedric straightened, realizing that the moment to intercede had arrived. But before he could speak, the door to the parlor was thrown open to reveal a tall, portly gentleman with gray hair and florid face. He stepped briskly into the room, and Cedric sighed at the sight of his aunt's brother. Although he loved Bartholomew Carson as dearly as he loved his aunt, he realized that Miss Cresswell was not about to be reassured by the owner of Mayford. In fact, he was quite certain that her faltering nerve was about to be shattered completely.

"Cassie, you must speak with those gardeners," he bellowed in the loud voice that had once commanded a thousand soldiers. "I will not have them searching for my treasure when my back is turned. Should have that beady-eyed one strung up by his toenails."

Unperturbed by the thunderous interruption, Lady Hartshore waved a delicate hand.

"Yes, yes, Bart, I will speak with them, but first I wish to introduce you to my new companion, Miss Cresswell."

Giving a grunt, Bart glanced over the stiffly silent Miss Cresswell.

"Companion, eh? About time. Deuced tired of searching for every fallal you lose around the house. Black Bart at your service."

"Black Bart . . ." Miss Cresswell's already pale face drained to a near white.

Bart readily performed a deep bow. "The pirate, don't you know."

Lady Hartshore smiled at her brother. "I was just telling Miss Cresswell how nice it will be to have a young person around the house."

"Aye. It has become devilishly quiet around here," Bart agreed.

Cedric watched carefully as Miss Cresswell clutched the folds of her skirt. He was not certain whether she was about to faint or flee.

"Actually, I am not certain if I—"

"Aunt Cassie," Cedric firmly intruded into her hesitant words. "Perhaps you would request Mrs. Borelli to bring in tea? I have been longing for her scones for days."

As expected, his aunt readily rose to her feet with a pleased expression.

"Of course, my dear. I do know how much you love scones."

"I'll be off as well," Bart stated in firm tones. "Can't trust them gardeners for a moment. Sly lot. Ought to be hung."

Together the brother and sister left the parlor, giving Cedric an opportunity to speak alone with Miss Cresswell.

Or at least attempt to speak with her, he silently corrected himself as he was stabbed by a glittering emerald gaze. She did not appear much in the mood for a reasonable discussion.

"Why did you not warn me?" she gritted out.

He shrugged as he crossed toward the sofa. "I wished you to meet my family without any preconceived notions."

"You mean that you did not wish to admit that your aunt speaks with ghosts and her brother believes he is a pirate."

Cedric's smile faded at her scathing tone. "They are somewhat eccentric."

"Somewhat?" She drew in a shaky breath. "I begin to wonder if I have arrived at Bedlam."

"They are also kind and always willing to help those in need," he pointed out in low tones.

She sniffed at his words. "Surely you could not expect a respectable maiden to remain in such a household?"

His features hardened at her sharp question. He might sympathize with her shock, but no one was allowed to insult his family. Despite their fancies, they were far more worthy than the vast majority of the *ton*. They held no false pretenses, they did not seek position or power, and most important, they used their fortune to help others rather than abusing the less fortunate to line their own coffers. He felt nothing but pride in calling them family.

"Allow me to tell you of these people you have so readily dismissed as mad, Miss Cresswell," he said in cold tones. "My aunt took me in after my utterly respectable parents abandoned me for the pleasures of society and were eventually killed by highwaymen. She devoted her entire life to providing me and every other child in the neighborhood every delight we could desire."

A rather defensive expression settled upon the strained features. "She speaks with ghosts."

Cedric shrugged. "Yes. After my uncle was thrown from his horse and his neck broken, Aunt Cassie nearly died from grief. It was only the belief that her true love was still a part of her life that she managed to find the strength to go on."

A hint of confusion darkened the emerald eyes before her well-trained defenses returned.

"And what of Mr. Carson?"

His gaze narrowed in a dangerous fashion. "Once Bart was the finest general this country has ever known. He was honored by the king for his bravery and skill upon the battlefield. It was only after being wounded in India that he developed a rather harmless belief that he was Black Bart. That does not make him crazy or evil. Indeed, I have nothing but the greatest respect for Bartholomew Carson."

"I still feel it would be best if I return to London," she at last muttered.

"Why?"

She faltered for a moment at his blunt attack.

"Your aunt has no need of a companion."

Although Cedric readily agreed with her logic, he was aware that his aunt had convinced herself that she was in need of Miss Cresswell's presence. If the maiden were to bolt, then Lady Hartshore would no doubt fret and stew herself into an illness.

And, of course, a tiny voice whispered in the back of his mind, he would be denied the pleasure of discovering the mystery she was attempting to hide.

"Perhaps not in the traditional sense," he agreed, "but I believe she would find a great deal of happiness in your presence."

She unconsciously licked her lips at his gentle pressure.

"I cannot simply remain here with no duties."

A wry smile softened his stern countenance.

"There are any number of duties you could perform, not the least of which is keeping track of the endless books, handkerchiefs, and needlework my aunt is constantly losing. And, of course, ensuring she recalls to eat at least one meal a day. She can be remarkably scatter-brained when it comes to the more mundane matters."

"A maid would surely do as well?"

"No," he firmly denied. "What she truly needs is someone to bear her company and allow her to fuss over them. She is lonely. Surely that is what a respectable companion is for?"

With a shaky motion she rose to her feet. Cedric closely studied her pale features. He could detect no deep-rooted fear of being in a haunted house or terror she might be murdered by a crazed pirate. Her urgency to leave seemed to have more to do with the thought of being in a household that might be considered strange.

"This is not what I was expecting," she muttered lowly.

Cedric felt a flare of rueful amusement. He was quite certain no maiden could have been expecting his aunt Cassie or Black Bart.

"Would you have preferred a sour old puss who treated you with the bitter contempt usually reserved for maidens in your position?" he asked softly.

Her hands unconsciously twisted together. "I just want a dull, predictable position among a dull, predictable family."

He moved closer to grasp her tangled fingers.

"A rather odd desire."

For once she did not immediately pull away and he hid an amused smile. She must be deeply disturbed not to recall she was supposed to dislike his touch.

"Not for me," she muttered.

"Miss Cresswell, allow me to offer you a proposition."

Her eyes widened at his soft tone. "No."

He was momentarily baffled by her fierce reaction,

then abruptly realizing that she had misinterpreted his request, he gave a low chuckle.

"Not that sort of proposition, my dear, although I will not deny that I would certainly be willing to discuss a more intimate arrangement should you desire," he assured her. "I was thinking more in terms of your position at Mayford."

The shock faded, but the wariness remained. "What?"

Cedric took a moment to consider his rash notion before giving an unconscious shrug. His aunt's happiness was of paramount importance.

"Remain for a month," he urged. "If at the end of that time you still desire to leave, then I shall pay you three months salary so that you are able to chose your next position with care."

She stilled as she reluctantly met his steady gaze. "Why do you wish me to remain?"

In truth Cedric was not certain that he wished to ponder the question too deeply. Instead, he audaciously trailed a finger down her satin cheek.

"Because Fredrick and Mrs. Borelli's tea leaves are never wrong."

Only moments later, Cedric tracked down his aunt just leaving the kitchen. He had been reluctant to leave Miss Cresswell, far from certain she would not flee Mayford the moment his back was turned. But the realization that he could not lock her in the cellar or compel her to stay had forced him to realize he had done all that he could for the moment. Perhaps it would be best to give her the opportunity to become acquainted with his aunt without his presence. A rueful smile touched his lips. Indeed, she would no doubt be much more inclined to remain without the unfortunate reminder he was a relative of Lady Hartshore's.

"Oh, Cedric," his aunt cried as she caught sight of his tall form. "Mrs. Borelli is just finishing the tea tray."

"I fear I must be returning home," he gently apologized.

"So soon?"

"Yes." He took a moment to study the tiny, birdlike features. "What do you think of Miss Cresswell?"

The gray head tilted. "She is very lovely."

He met the deceptively innocent expression with a wry smile. "Yes, I had noticed."

"Mmm . . . I thought you had."

Not about to be distracted by thoughts of Miss Cresswell's loveliness or the pleasure of her lips, Cedric returned the conversation to the issue at hand.

"Are you certain you wish her to stay?"

"But of course," Cassie answered with a hint of surprise. "Fredrick was most insistent."

And that, of course, settled the matter, he inwardly sighed.

"I do not suppose he has told you why Miss Cresswell should be at Mayford?"

She waved a chiding finger in his direction. "You know he cannot tell me the future. I believe it must be against the rules."

"Rules among the netherworld?" he teased.

"Of course. Spirits cannot simply flutter about, doing as they please."

Cedric had to laugh at the sheer absurdity. "Indeed not. All those ghosts rattling around with no direction."

"You are quizzing me."

"Perhaps a bit."

Cassie remained undisturbed by his teasing. "Fredrick is never wrong. At least since he has passed to the other side."

Cedric was in no position to refute such a claim, since his uncle deigned to speak only with his wife, but his concern did not lay with the long-departed Lord Hartshore.

"Perhaps not, but I do feel it incumbent upon me to warn you that there is every likelihood Miss Cresswell will flee back to London at the first opportunity."

She met his gaze squarely. "Then we must endeavor to keep her here. At least until we discover why she is needed."

Cedric grimaced, thinking of Miss Cresswell's stubborn nature. "That is no doubt easier said than done."

"We shall find some means."

He felt a familiar flare of rueful amusement at his aunt's blithe confidence in fate.

"What an incurable optimist you are. I do hope that Miss Cresswell will not disappoint you."

She searched his countenance at his low words. "Do you not like her?"

He slowly crossed his arms over his chest. "On the contrary, I find her utterly fascinating."

"What do you mean?"

"I mean that I wonder why a well-educated, well-dressed maiden with a veritable fortune hung around her neck would chose to become your companion. And why she is so frightened to enjoy her life."

"We shall discover the truth in time."

Cedric gave a slow nod. "Yes."

"And she will certainly add a bit of gaiety to this dismal winter," Cassie continued. "I dearly love Bart, but he is not the best of company."

"As long as you are not too disappointed if you awaken and discover that she has bolted," he warned, knowing how swiftly his aunt became attached to those around her.

She reached up to gently pat his cheek. "All will be well, I am certain."

Cedric captured her hand. "I do hope you are right. You mean a great deal to me, my dearest."

A smile lit her tiny features. "You are a good boy."

Cedric gave a sudden chuckle. "Actually I have recently been informed that I am a lecher of helpless ladies, annoying, an arrogant beast, and a rogue."

"Nonsense," Cassie loyally denied.

Giving the hand a light kiss, Cedric stepped back. "Take care of my wood nymph. I shall return on the morrow."

Four

Emma awoke the next morning to discover that her ankle was much improved. Unfortunately her head was thick and faintly throbbing from a sleepless night.

For hours she had tossed across the vast bed, struggling with the decision that lay before her.

She did not want to remain at Mayford, she told herself. How could she? The entire household was batty. Ghosts and pirates and fortune-tellers . . . it was absurd. A respectable maiden would not remain. Not only would she be distinctly uncomfortable, but what other matron would hire her after discovering she had been in the employ of such a family?

And, of course, there was the disturbing knowledge that Lord Hartshore would be far too close for comfort.

The man was a menace, she brooded. From the moment he had appeared standing over her like a dark angel, he had bullied, charmed, and unnerved her. And as for his kisses . . . well, that was something best not dwelt upon.

How could she possibly endure the knowledge he might appear at any moment? She would be a twittering ball of nerves by the time she left Kent.

Then, as swiftly as those thoughts would flood through her mind, a more rational voice would abruptly intrude.

How could she simply leave?

She had arrived in Kent with only a few quid in her pocket. Certainly she did not possess enough to purchase a ticket back to London. And she could hardly expect Lady Hartshore to bear the expense or to send her in her own carriage. Even supposing Emma would consent to risking her neck to the unpredictable driving of James.

And supposing she did manage to make her way back to London? She had no position awaiting her. She would once again be forced to depend upon Sarah for support until she could find new employment.

Why not accept Lord Hartshore's proposition? the voice had whispered.

One month would swiftly pass and then she would be free to leave with enough money to tide her over until she could find a more proper position.

All night she had argued back and forth, torn between the indefinable fear of remaining and the knowledge it would be foolish to flee.

At last, as dawn crept into the pretty rose-and-ivory chamber, she made her decision.

She would remain at Mayford for one month.

After that she would flee from this madhouse with all possible speed.

Climbing from her bed, she dressed in a sensible gray gown and smoothed her hair to a tidy bun. Then accepting she was as prepared as she ever would be, she forced herself to leave her chambers and wend her way the long distance back to the main hall.

It was only as she hovered in the gallery that she realized she hadn't the least notion of what she should be doing. Lady Hartshore had firmly refused to discuss her duties, and without knowledge of the household's normal routine she could not presume to guess how best to begin her service.

Was Lady Hartshore an early riser and already bus-

tling about her morning routine? Or did she prefer to
linger in her chambers until a more fashionable hour?

She was busily debating whether to simply await Lady
Hartshore in the parlor or to seek her out, when the
sound of approaching footsteps made her sigh in relief.
Surely whoever was approaching could give her some
hint of where Lady Hartshore could be found.

Turning, she waited until a large form appeared. She
felt her heart sink as she realized it was Mr. Carson. For
all her sister's training on how to comport herself as a
lady, Emma was uncertain how one was to behave toward
a pirate.

With an effort she managed a smile as Bart came to
a halt beside her and offered a faint bow.

"Hello, hello," he boomed in his loud voice. "Looking
for the galley?"

"Good morning, Mr. Carson."

"Black Bart will do, missy."

"Uh . . . yes." She determinedly held on to her smile.
"I was searching for Lady Hartshore."

The gray brows shot upward. "Lost, is she? Typical
of Cassie, I fear. Kind as a lamb, but no sense to speak
of. Bird-witted, that's the trouble."

"No, I did not mean that she was lost," she hastily
attempted to clarify. "I meant only that I wished to speak
with her."

"Oh."

"Do you know where she might be this morning?"

Surprisingly, her timid question appeared to ruffle his
good humor.

" 'Course I know. I ain't daft no matter what those
devils might say behind my back."

Emma swallowed an urge to smile. So Bart was not
as indifferent to the world around him as others might
believe, she silently acknowledged.

"Could you tell me where to find her?"

"In the kitchen, where she is every morning."

Emma gave a faint frown, certain the gentleman had made a mistake.

"Do you mean the breakfast room?"

"Egads, no," he protested with some force. "Can't cook up food and serve it to every wretch who comes by from the breakfast room. Not as long as I'm captain of this ship. No, I told Cassie when she come to me with the notion of filling this house with every scamp and scoundrel who offers her a sad tale that I won't have it. They can come to the back door and get their food and move along. Ain't no poorhouse."

Emma hadn't the slightest notion what he was speaking about, but she did gather that Lady Hartshore was indeed in the kitchen. Eager to locate the woman and sort out her day, Emma gave a small dip.

"Thank you."

"I'm off to the west woods," he announced as he held up a small spade. "Keep an eye on those gardeners for me, miss. A sly lot that has their eyes on my treasure."

"Yes, I will," she weakly agreed, uncertain what else to say.

"Glad to have you aboard."

With the precision that spoke of his military training, Mr. Carson turned on his heel and continued down the hall.

Emma gave a shake of her head as she altered her own course to take her toward the back of the house. Although she found the gentleman disconcerting, there was none of the fear she had expected at being alone with him. Perhaps because she had sensed beneath his bluster he was inherently kind, she decided. It was a pity his brilliant career had been marred by such an odd affliction.

Leaving behind the vaulted elegance of the house proper, Emma followed the distant sound of voices until she at last stepped into the large kitchen. She was not surprised to discover it a bustle of activity. As a governess, she had often witnessed life below stairs and knew that a great house required a vast amount of labor to keep it running smoothly. She was surprised, however, to discover Lady Hartshore covered in an apron as she pulled several loaves of perfectly browned bread from the oven.

Her brows unknowingly rose as the Countess of Hartshore expertly stacked the loaves on the counter and a large, dark-haired woman slid another tray of dough into the oven. They worked in a symphony of ease that assured Emma this was not the first occasion that Lady Hartshore had ventured into the kitchen.

"I believe we will add another loaf of bread and an extra meat pie in the basket for the Colberts, Mrs. Borelli," Lady Hartshore happily chattered. "They have eight children to feed now that Robert has returned home with his young ones."

"And perhaps some peach tarts?" Mrs. Borelli suggested.

"Lovely." Finished with the bread, Lady Hartshore glanced up to discover Emma standing in the doorway. A charming smile that was disturbingly similar to her nephew's curved her lips as she bustled forward. "My dear, I did not imagine you to be such an early riser."

Emma felt a prick of guilt as she guessed that the older woman had no doubt been up for some time. Although she was not thoroughly acquainted with the expectations of a companion, she was certain that most did not lie abed while her employer toiled in the kitchen.

"I assure you that I am usually up quite early," she attempted to reassure the countess. "You must think me the most wretched slugabed."

"Nonsense, my dear. I am delighted to see you are not nearly so pale."

Emma was relieved that her restless sleep was not visible on her countenance. She had no desire to confess what had kept her staring at the ceiling far into the night.

"No, I am quite rested," she said with more enthusiasm than truth.

"And famished, I am certain. Mrs. Borelli will see to your breakfast."

Accustomed to employers who considered her basic needs a necessary evil to be overlooked whenever possible, Emma gave a swift shake of her head.

"Oh, no. A bit of toast and tea will do nicely." She glanced toward the food piled onto the large wooden table. "You appear to be very busy this morning."

Lady Hartshore heaved a sigh. "So many mouths to feed."

The heavyset cook closed the oven door. "Likely to have thirty or better this morning. Winter is a poor time to be hungry."

Emma couldn't imagine there was ever a good time to be hungry.

"Oh, yes, that reminds me." Lady Hartshore turned to her cook. "Has John stacked the coal outside?"

"Aye, he did it afore sunup."

"Good. Now, where was I?" The older woman tapped a finger to her chin, then, as a knock sounded on the nearby door, she flashed the puzzled Emma a sudden smile. "That will be the first. Miss Cresswell, could I prevail upon you to stand beside the table and hand me the food as we need it?"

Still wondering if there was ever a normal moment in this odd house, Emma obligingly moved to stand beside the table. She shivered as the door was pulled open and a young woman with several children clutched to her rough cloak stepped into the kitchen. Taking the basket that she held in her hand, Lady Hartshore directed Emma to fill it with several meat pies, a loaf of bread, and a jug of fresh cream. She then turned to hand it to the young woman, who offered a weary smile. With a skill that Emma could only admire, Lady Hartshore averted the woman's halting words of thanks, her brisk manner ensuring there was no awkwardness as the young family turned from the door and was immediately replaced by an elderly man with an obvious limp.

For the next hour Emma was kept hustling from the table to the oven, where Mrs. Borelli was creating her magic. She had swiftly lost her initial shock that a countess would toss aside her dignity and play the role of a common kitchen-maid. The overwhelming gratitude and relief on the countless faces that appeared at the door was proof that her kindly efforts were of far greater importance than the pomp and ceremony of a more traditional countess.

In many ways the woman reminded Emma of her older sister, Sarah. There was the same overwhelming need to improve the lives of others, the same skill in avoiding the awkward embarrassment of those receiving their charity, and the same lack of regard for what others might think of her efforts.

Indeed, Emma wryly acknowledged, if Lady Hartshore and Sarah ever became acquainted, society might be rocked to its very foundation.

Feeling somewhat weary but surprisingly pleased that she had been a small part of ensuring so many families would go to bed with full stomachs, she brushed back a honey curl that had strayed from her rigid bun.

"Goodness, do you do this every morning?" she asked with a hint of amazement.

Lady Hartshore brushed back her own scattered curls, leaving a trace of flour on her flushed cheek.

"Yes, but you needn't suppose that you are obliged to become part of our madness," she assured her with a small laugh. "If you prefer, you could have a nice breakfast in bed."

"Oh, no, I would prefer to help. But . . ." Emma gave a lift of her slender hands. "Who are these people?"

"Many are from the village, and a few are tenants who have fallen upon hard times," Lady Hartshore explained, her eyes revealing a deep concern for those who came to her door. "And, of course, there are those strangers who have heard of our small efforts and merely appear."

"We turn no one away," Mrs. Borelli added in proud tones. "Unlike that rotter of a vicar."

"Mrs. Borelli," the countess protested.

"It be true enough," the cook insisted without apology. In the past hour Emma had discovered the large woman who claimed to be of Gypsy blood often spoke her mind with little consideration to her station in the household. Not that Lady Hartshore appeared to mind, Emma acknowledged with a wry sigh. "Giving himself airs and not wishing to soil his lily-white hands with the common folk. Might as well have a toadstool at the vicarage."

Lady Hartshore heaved a regretful sigh. "It is true that he concerns himself more with those of position than those in need."

Mrs. Borelli gave a loud snort, her hands already busy sorting through the basket of vegetables that had just arrived from the hothouses.

"Good for nothing more than prosy speeches and condemning those beneath him. Not at all like Mr. Galloway."

"Well, we must make do with what we have," Lady Hartshore attempted to console.

The cook reached for a cleaver and chopped a carrot in half with enough force to make Emma blink in surprise.

"A sad day when he arrived," the cook muttered.

Clearly more accustomed to the woman's habit of

venting her displeasure upon hapless vegetables, Lady Hartshore sent Emma a rueful grimace.

"I fear Mrs. Borelli is somewhat prejudiced. Mr. Allensway has condemned her fortune telling as the work of the devil."

The cleaver slammed through a potato.

"A God-given gift is what it is," Mrs. Borelli muttered. "A blessing."

"Yes, we all believe so," Lady Hartshore soothed, moving to link arms with the wary Emma. "Now, we shall leave you to get on with lunch."

Quite willing to leave the company of the cleaver-toting cook, Emma was nevertheless compelled to halt Lady Hartshore from sweeping her from the kitchen.

"A moment, Lady Hartshore."

"Yes, my dear?"

"Your apron."

"Oh, yes." Lady Hartshore gave a tinkling laugh as she struggled out of the voluminous garment. "Bless you, my dear."

"And you have some flour . . ." Emma reached out to brush away the fine white powder.

Once again claiming Emma's arm, Lady Hartshore smiled happily and led them from the kitchen.

"There, I knew you should be invaluable."

"I have yet to do anything."

"Nonsense." Lady Hartshore squeezed her arm as they continued toward the main house. "You have already brightened this quiet household."

Emma gave a wry shake of her head, wondering what the older woman would think if she informed her that she was accustomed to waking at dawn and working until the children were at last asleep. And that even then she was expected to finish the mending or to embroider upon one of Mrs. Falwell's gowns.

The kindly woman would no doubt be horrified if

Emma suggested that she provide her with a list of duties each morning.

They stepped into the long hall, and Emma's rueful thoughts were scattered as she caught sight of the sun-drenched parkland visible beyond the long stretch of arched windows.

When she had arrived in Kent she had been cold, frightened, and unnerved by the fog-shrouded landscape. Now, for the first time, she noted the majestic beauty of the rustic gardens, the sparkling lake with its charming grotto, and the nearby woods.

True there was none of the vibrant color and sounds of a bustling city. But there was something very peaceful and charming in the pristine solitude.

Barely aware she had halted, Emma regarded the scene with a peculiar sense of wonder.

"What a lovely view," she murmured.

Seemingly content to linger, Lady Hartshore regarded her in a quizzical manner.

"Is this your first visit to Kent?"

"Yes."

"Oh, my dear, we must see the sights," the older woman declared in firm tones.

Emma turned toward her with a rise of her brows. "Sights?"

"Yes, indeed." Lady Hartshore gave a firm nod of her head. "There is Heaver Castle, which you know was once the home of poor Anne Boleyn. Such lovely gardens. And Penhurst Place, which belongs to the Sidneys. It has a chestnut-beamed roof, which is quite worth the trip. And, of course, there is Leeds Castle. It is set in the middle of a lake. Quite breathtaking. Elizabeth was imprisoned there, or at least she was until her coronation."

Emma felt a small thrill of anticipation at the thought of viewing the historical structures that she had only read of in books before she was sternly suppressing the renegade emotion.

She was not there to sightsee.

"You mustn't treat me as a guest," she insisted in firm tones. "I am here to help you."

Lady Hartshore gave a click of her tongue. "Nonsense. You are my guest. A most welcome guest."

Emma bit back her words of denial. What was the point? She could clearly not alter Lady Hartshore's refusal to see her as a servant.

The important thing was that she never forget her position at Mayford, she told herself sternly.

It would be far too easy to be seduced into taking advantage of Lady Hartshore's kindness. After the Falwells' disparaging dislike, the sense of warm welcome was a refreshing balm to her heart. But she would be a fool to become accustomed to such friendliness. And an even bigger fool to allow herself to become in any way attached to Lady Hartshore.

In one month she would be leaving. She did not want any complications.

"You are too kind," she at last murmured.

"Not really," Lady Hartshore denied with a twinkle in her eye. "To be truthful, I am being very selfish. I always wished to have a daughter, and now I shall indulge myself."

Emma bit her lip as she turned her blurred gaze back to the window. She would not be swayed, she told herself. She already possessed one unconventional, unpredictable, utterly scandalous family. She did not seek to become a part of another.

"You have no children?"

Lady Hartshore heaved a sigh. "No, Lord Hartshore and I were never blessed. Although Cedric is as much a son as if he were my own. His parents died when he was quite young, poor dear."

Parents who had chosen a life among society rather than with their own son, Emma recalled Lord Hartshore's dark words.

"Yes, he mentioned that you raised him."

"Such a wonderful boy. It was difficult for him to step into Fredrick's position after his death. They were so very close. But he has managed remarkably well. The tenants adore him and he is very shrewd in business matters. More shrewd than Fredrick, who, I must admit, was forever in the stables rather than his study."

"Yes, I am certain he is very competent," she forced herself to agree.

Despite her best effort, a hint of her annoyance must have been obvious in her tone, and Lady Hartshore gave a small chuckle.

"You mustn't mind his teasing, my dear. Cedric has always found the world a very amusing place and presumes that others share his sense of humor."

Emma sternly refused to allow the image of devilish golden eyes and an annoyingly charming smile to rise to mind.

"Yes," she said stiffly.

As if sensing Emma's reluctance to discuss the roguish Lord Hartshore, the older woman once again linked arms with Emma and began leading her down the hall.

"Now, tell me of your family," she chattered, unaware that her delicate shift of conversation did little to ease Emma's discomfort. "I suppose your parents were very sad to have you travel so far away."

Retreating behind her well-trained defenses, Emma gave a faint shrug.

"Actually my mother died when I was quite young, and I am not close to my father."

"Oh . . . I am so sorry, my dear," Lady Hartshore exclaimed with genuine sympathy. "How dreadful for you."

"Oh, no, I've always had my sisters, Sarah and Rachel. They are a comfort to me."

Lady Hartshore patted her hand. "You must feel free to invite them to stay at Mayford. It would be a delight to have them here."

"Perhaps," Emma temporized, knowing she would not be in Kent long enough for any visits, even should she be inclined to extend the offer.

In a companionable silence they continued their way back toward the front parlor, the faint swish of their skirts the only sound to disturb the hushed silence. Emma discovered her tension fading as her gaze skimmed over the exquisite tapestries and gilt gesso chairs that lined the hall. For all the sprawling grandeur of Mayford, Lady Hartshore had managed to create a warmth that was a welcome surprise in such a vast establishment.

Emma halted as Lady Hartshore pushed open the door, then, stepping into the parlor, she halted again, her heart giving a startled jolt at the sight of the tall gentleman standing beside the fire.

Throughout the long night Emma had deliberately kept her thoughts far away from Lord Hartshore. She had known that to dwell upon his disturbing presence would certainly send her fleeing from Mayford. Now she encountered that glittering golden gaze with considerable trepidation.

"Cedric," Lady Hartshore cried at her side. "I did not realize you were here."

"I asked Mallory not to disturb you. I know how busy your mornings can be."

"Oh, yes, it was quite hectic. Thankfully Miss Cresswell proved to be a valuable ally."

"I am not at all surprised." Lord Hartshore turned his attention to the silent Emma. "I do hope your ankle is improved?"

"Very much, thank you."

"What brings you to Mayford, my dear?" Lady Hartshore demanded.

"Actually I wished to speak with Miss Cresswell," he admitted in blunt tones.

Emma stiffened, but Lady Hartshore seemed to find nothing peculiar in his request to speak with her companion. Indeed, a most worrisome smile suddenly curved her lips.

"Oh, I see. Well, I shall ensure that Bart is not disturbing the gardeners. He does not comprehend how difficult it is to keep dependable servants."

Emma waited in rigid silence as Lady Hartshore swept from the room and even went so far as to shut the door behind her.

Traitor, she thought as Lord Hartshore slowly strolled toward her.

Against her will she was once again struck by just how astonishingly handsome this man was. Although his buckskins and deep green coat were more casual than she was accustomed to in the city, they were fitted with spectacular precision to reveal every lean muscle.

Far too many lean muscles, she acknowledged before jerking her gaze to the dark, exquisitely carved features.

As if sensing her embarrassing awareness of his decidedly male body, Lord Hartshore deliberately did not halt until he was standing far too close.

"Did you sleep well?" he asked softly, no doubt well aware she had lain awake all night.

His warm, sweet breath brushed her cheek, and it was only stubborn pride that kept her from backing from his looming form.

"Well enough."

"You at least have some color in your cheeks."

Dratted man. He must know that it was his presence putting color in her cheeks.

"Why did you wish to speak with me?"

"Can we have a seat?"

She paused, then gave a small shrug. "If you wish."

He stood aside to allow her to precede him to the sofa, then, waiting for her to perch stiffly on the edge, he lowered himself next to her. Unlike her, however, he lounged back in perfect ease.

"You needn't perch on the edge of the cushion, Miss Cresswell. I am not about to pounce."

She regarded him sourly. "After our last encounter, I can hardly be expected to know what you intend."

"I must protest, my dear." The golden eyes sparkled. "I did not pounce. I merely took advantage of a fortunate situation."

"Fortunate for you perhaps."

"Oh, yes, very fortunate." He carefully watched the fine shiver that she could not prevent before giving a small laugh. "However, today I desire nothing more scandalous than a polite conversation. Surely not even you can find fault with such an innocent request?"

Five

Cedric had faithfully promised himself that he would not attempt to provoke Miss Cresswell.

After all, he had half expected to arrive at Mayford to discover she had vanished into the mist. When he was assured that she was still in residence, he had silently warned himself not to give her cause to bolt.

Unfortunately his good intentions had disappeared as swiftly as lobster patties upon Prinny's plate.

And who could blame him?

What gentleman could resist bringing a sparkle to those magnificent eyes and a blush to her cheeks? That brittle composure she shrouded around herself was an insult to the warm woman beneath.

She should be filled with laughter and the simple delight of being alive. Not so tightly clenched that she appeared she might crack beneath the burdens she carried deep inside.

Carefully studying the stiff lines of her features, he watched her sternly smother her shiver of awareness behind a pretense of indifference.

"A conversation with you is rarely innocent, my lord."

His lips twitched. "I assure you that I can be the very model of a proper gentleman when I choose."

"Why do you suppose I find that difficult to believe?" she said dryly.

"I haven't the least notion. You have only to ask my aunt. She will assure you that I am above reproach."

A hint of exasperated amusement could be detected deep in her eyes. "She could hardly say otherwise."

"Perhaps," Cedric agreed, then he gave a faint tilt of his head. "What do you think of her?"

There was a moment's pause, as if she considered lying, then apparently realizing that no one with a breath of sense would believe Lady Hartshore was anything but adorable, she gave a shrug.

"She is very kind."

"Yes, she is." Cedric slowly leaned forward to peer deep into her eyes. "She is also patient, loyal, and very generous. I cannot imagine a finer woman."

Unable to deny the truth of his words, she abruptly lowered her gaze.

"Is that what you wished to discuss with me?"

With her gaze averted, Cedric was allowed to openly study the pale, nearly translucent skin that was stretched over the delicate bones of her face. It was a skin that begged for a man's touch.

His touch.

It took a surprising effort to keep his hands from rising to trace the line of her cheek and press the lush fullness of her lips.

Provoking a glitter to her eyes was one thing, pulling her in his arms and ravishing her on the settee was quite another.

"In a manner of speaking." He forced himself to concentrate on the reason for his visit. Although ravishing her on the sofa was a far more tantalizing reason for visiting, he acknowledged ruefully. "Have you given any thought to my proposition?"

Her hands clenched on her lap. "Of course."

"You will stay?" he asked softly.

She sucked in a deep breath before reluctantly lifting her gaze. "I agree to remain one month."

Cedric smiled as he released the breath he did not even realize he had been holding.

"I hoped you would say that."

Her own expression remained guarded. "You will still have to find a new companion."

Cedric's smile never faltered. He had won the first skirmish. She had given her promise to remain a month. He did not doubt she would remain faithful to that vow.

"Perhaps. Or perhaps you will fall in love with Kent and never wish to leave."

Surprisingly her eyes darkened at his teasing words. "No."

His brows rose at the odd edge in her tone. "How can you be so certain? Unless you can read the future like Mrs. Borelli?"

"If I could read the future, I would never have gotten into the coach with a drunken groom," she pointed out in tart tones.

Cedric chuckled at her sharp wit. There was an intelligence behind those pretty features.

"No, I daresay you would not have," he agreed. "Poor James feels quite wretched. He wished to seek you out and apologize, but I convinced him to wait until you were not so eager to throttle him."

"I have no intention of throttling him," she denied.

"No, your weapon of choice is that wicked tongue of yours," he retorted softly. "And a most potent weapon it is."

"Are you ever serious, my lord?" she demanded with a shake of her head.

Cedric pondered her words a moment. It was true that he preferred a good laugh over a glass of ale to poring through musty tomes of the philosophers. And while other landowners might form a committee to discuss the heavy burden of the poor or the local politics, he preferred to stand beside his tenants as they repaired the roof to their cottage or hauled their wares to the market.

That did not mean he did not care for others. He merely possessed his own means of expressing that concern.

"At times," he at last conceded, "but life is too short not to enjoy. If I die tomorrow I wish it to be with the knowledge I appreciated every moment." He regarded her with a curious expression. "What of you?"

She was caught off guard as he neatly turned the tables on her.

"What do you mean?"

"Is there nothing you enjoy?"

"Of course. I enjoy reading and needlework and . . ."

He gave an impatient click of his tongue. He would not be satisfied with the vague platitudes that she offered to the rest of the world. He wanted to know what she thought, what she felt, and most important, what she was hiding from.

"I do not mean what you do to pass the time. What makes you happy?"

"Many things."

"Such as what?" he demanded, keeping her gaze locked with his own. "Walking in the rain? Watching a child play? Seeing the sunrise? Being close to someone you love?"

He could visibly see her retreat from his probing.

"I am not here to enjoy myself, my lord. I am here to work."

Cedric was unimpressed by her fierce words. It might be an admirable sentiment, but he suspected it was merely an excuse.

"You surely have deduced that you will never be treated as a servant at Mayford? My aunt considers all here as her friends."

Her lips thinned. "I am determined not to take advantage of her kindness."

"A wasted effort, my dear," he drawled. "Why not simply enjoy your time in Kent? As you have so firmly determined to seek another position, you will soon enough be among those who regard you as another piece of property."

Just for a moment he thought he had actually struck a nerve, then she was giving a faint shake of her head.

"I cannot accept your money without performing some duties, my lord."

Cedric heaved a sigh. His aunt had always assured him that the things most difficult to achieve were always the most worthwhile.

Miss Emma Cresswell must be worthwhile, indeed.

"Very well, my stubborn wood nymph."

"Please do not call me that," she muttered in low tones.

"Why?" He leaned close enough to smell the soap clinging to her porcelain skin. It was a scent that was oddly enticing. Far more enticing than heavy perfume and oils. "It is how I think of you."

Her eyes widened. "You should not be thinking of me at all."

The sheer absurdity of her prim words made Cedric give a disbelieving laugh.

"You might as well request the sun not to rise tomorrow. Or the stars not to twinkle in a midnight sky. It is an impossible task."

She threw up her hands at his deliberately trite words, but he did not miss the revealing twitch of her lips.

"You are impossible."

"And you almost smiled," he said gently.

The long lashes fluttered. "I—" Her flustered words were abruptly cut off as a shrill scream echoed through the air, followed by the unmistakable sound of running footsteps. "What is that?"

As confused as Miss Cresswell, Cedric rose to his feet. At the same moment the door to the parlor was thrown open and a thin gentleman attired in black rushed into the room. With obvious agitation the intruder slammed the door shut behind him and leaned against it as he struggled to regain his breath.

"My lord, you must save me," he panted.

Cedric's astonishment faded to annoyance as he studied the familiar features and thatch of brown hair that was currently standing on end.

Good gads, it was bad enough to have his delightful interlude with Miss Cresswell interrupted. To have it interrupted by a pompous, self-absorbed vicar made his teeth clench.

"What the devil do you mean, bursting into a room unannounced, Mr. Allensway?" he demanded in cold tones.

"That . . . witch was chasing me with a carving knife. You must do something about her."

The pieces fell into place as Cedric realized the vicar must have crossed paths with his aunt's volatile cook. Although there were many in the neighborhood who would gladly throttle the irritating gentleman, Mrs. Borelli was the only one who had actually threatened to slice him open.

"I suppose you are referring to Mrs. Borelli?"

"Of course I am," Mr. Allensway sputtered, a dark flush marring his pointed features. "The woman should be locked away."

Cedric crossed his arms over his chest as he peered down his long nose.

"Do not be daft. She creates the most divine trout in cream sauce."

Mr. Allensway's mouth opened and closed like a fish out of water.

"She attempted to kill me with a carving knife."

"Fah." Cedric was supremely indifferent to the vicar's hysteria. "Had she intended to kill you, she would most certainly have chosen a cleaver."

Cedric heard a choked sound from the woman still seated on the settee. He suspected that it might have been a laugh, although it was swiftly hidden behind a cough. Mr. Allensway, on the other hand, clearly found nothing humorous about his smooth dismissal. Pushing away from the door, he gave a loud sniff.

"Surely you do not find this amusing, my lord?" he accused in sharp tones. "That fiend should be handed over to the magistrate."

Cedric's eyes narrowed in a dangerous manner. "That fiend is a perfectly lovely woman who simply dislikes being branded a witch. As would anyone."

Thoroughly unrepentant at the knowledge he had deliberately attempted to destroy a harmless woman, he pursed his thin lips.

"She practices barbarian rituals that are an affront to God."

"And did God personally tell you he was affronted? Or did you simply presume that he should be?"

The sniff came again, only louder. "I am merely doing my duty."

Cedric longed to tell the man he hoped he choked on his vindictive devotion to duty, but realizing it would be nothing more than a waste of breath, he instead attempted to rid himself of his aggravating presence.

"Did you possess a purpose in coming to Mayford other than insulting my aunt's cook?"

As if on cue, the thin features abruptly shifted from a petulant frown to a forced smile. Cedric knew that smile. He was quite certain that his sunny disposition was about to be strained to the very limit.

"Of course, my lord." Mr. Allensway reached up to pat his rumpled cravat. "I have received a missive from the bishop that I am to expect a guest within the next fortnight."

"Indeed?"

Ignoring Cedric's less than encouraging tone, the vicar gave another pat to his cravat. "Well, to be honest, I have been expecting such a development for some months. After all, the bishop is bound to have heard of my many charitable efforts throughout the neighborhood and, of course, my determination to put an end to the archaic beliefs that the lower class is so prone to cling to. It was only a matter of time before I was considered for a more respectable position."

It was a testament to his aunt's training that Cedric did not double over in laughter. The closest the man had come to charitable efforts was to accidentally drop a bread crumb while consuming his dinner. And as for putting an end to archaic beliefs . . . well, if shrilly accusing good people of performing works of the devil and driving them from the church was putting an end to archaic beliefs, then he was indeed a resounding success.

Certainly, no respectable bishop would consider this gentleman as anything more than a buffoon.

"And this visitor is coming to offer you such a position?" he asked in disbelief.

"The bishop, of course, is not so crude as to do more than hint at the truth. He says that Mr. Winchell is a close friend and that I should introduce him to the neighborhood. One must read between the lines to discern the full meaning."

"You must be very adept at reading between the lines," Cedric retorted in dry tones.

The vicar preened in a smug manner. "As you know,

my lord, gentlemen in our positions are naturally gifted with such talents."

Gentlemen in their position? Cedric shuddered.

"What is it that you want from my aunt?"

"Ah . . . yes." Mr. Allensway cleared his throat. "It is clearly of the utmost importance that Mr. Winchell receive a favorable impression of my efforts. Particularly among those of superior social standing."

Cedric grimaced. "And you desire me to sing your praises?"

"Well, I would not be averse to a kindly placed word, of course," the vicar readily encouraged. "However, my reason for coming concerns Lady Hartshore and Mr. Carson."

Cedric felt his muscles stiffen. This man had condemned his aunt as a lunatic and Bart as a danger to the neighborhood. It was only because he hid behind his position as a man of God that Cedric had not already bloodied his nose.

"I see," he said, his voice a quiet threat.

Impervious to the danger in the air, Mr. Allensway smiled in a patronizing manner.

"Although I am, of course, very fond of Lady Hartshore and her brother, their odd behavior is bound to shock any God-fearing gentleman. I hope you will encourage them to behave in a circumspect manner when in the company of Mr. Winchell."

Cedric thought he heard a faint gasp from behind him, but his attention remained firmly centered upon the vicar.

"Circumspect?"

Mr. Allensway gave a lift of his hands. "In a manner more fitted to their position."

Sheer fury flared through Cedric. Why, the vain, annoying little twit!

"I suggest, Mr. Allensway, that you take leave of Mayford with all possible speed," he said in clipped tones.

"But, my lord . . ."

"Now."

"If you would just mention it to Lady Hartshore."

"You have to the count of ten to be out of my sight, Mr. Allensway."

"But . . ."

"One, two, three . . ."

This time not even the supremely dense vicar could miss the danger lying thick in the air.

Hastily pulling open the door, he gave a jerky bow. "As you wish, my lord."

Still bent over, he backed into the hall and hurriedly closed the door, nearly catching his pointed nose in the process. Clearly his fear of the murderous cook had suddenly been overcome by an even more potent fear.

Glaring at the closed door, Cedric resisted the urge to follow the man and physically toss him from the estate.

"One day I shall take great delight in throttling that puffed-up fool," he muttered, then, realizing he had allowed his anger to overcome his good manners, he slowly turned to regard the silent Miss Cresswell with a wry smile. If she wasn't certain that she had landed in Bedlam before, this morning should have convinced her.

It wasn't every household that possessed a cook who chased vicars through the halls with a carving knife. Nor a lord who threatened to throttle his guests.

"Forgive me, Miss Cresswell. Mr. Allensway seems to possess an alarming ability to rile my temper."

Her expression was impossible to read as she slowly rose to her feet.

"Perhaps I should join Lady Hartshore."

Unwilling to allow the rare moment alone with this maiden to come to an end, Cedric reached out to place a restraining hand on her arm.

"Hold a moment."

She instinctively stepped from his touch. "What?"

"I brought you a surprise."

He moved toward the mantel even as he heard her give a choked sound.

"No . . . you should not have," she stammered, then, as he picked up his trifling gift and turned to reveal it to her, she gave a faint gasp. "Oh."

Decidedly pleased by the sudden hint of color in her cheeks, Cedric retraced his steps so he could press the dusky pink rose into her slender fingers.

"Do you like it?"

She slowly lifted the flower to sniff its heady aroma. Cedric felt a sharp stir of desire as the soft petals brushed her mouth. Good heavens, where had the image of her laid upon his bed, covered in nothing more than rose petals, come from? All he knew was that the sudden image was doing very dangerous things to his lower body.

"It is beautiful," she murmured.

With an effort Cedric reined in his delicious but highly improper thoughts.

"It is my own hybrid."

His soft words appeared to catch her off guard.

"You created this?"

He smiled. "With a little help from God."

"How lovely."

"I have been seeking the perfect name," he confessed as he stepped even closer to her slender form. "This morning it at last came to me."

For once she did not scurry from his proximity.

"What is it?"

"Wood nymph."

Her breath caught. "Oh."

Pleased with her ill-concealed pleasure, Cedric gently brushed her cheek.

"Do you approve?"

For a breathless moment her features softened, and he

realized he had slipped past her brittle facade. Then, with the most wretched timing, the door to the parlor was thrown open and his aunt stepped into the room.

"Fredrick told me that the vicar is here," she claimed in dramatic tones.

Muffling a frustrated curse, Cedric watched the stoic composure stiffen Miss Cresswell's features. Blast his deceased uncle. Why did he not rattle chains and float around the attic like other self-respecting ghosts? His habit of chattering like a magpie to his wife was creating all sorts of trouble.

With a faint sigh, Cedric turned toward his aunt, knowing whatever progress he had made with Miss Cresswell was now lost.

"Do not fear. I have already sent him on his way," he assured the older woman.

Lady Hartshore gave a shake of her head. "I wish he would not visit. It is very upsetting for Mrs. Borelli."

Cedric grimaced, knowing that while he had rid them of the vicar for the moment, it was only a temporary reprieve.

"I fear that we will be seeing a good deal of Mr. Allensway over the next several weeks. He has a visitor arriving whom he hopes to impress."

"Oh, dear." His aunt pressed a hand to her bosom. "I do hope that nothing untoward occurs."

"I will speak with Mrs. Borelli and request that she keep her knives sheathed," he promised.

"Yes, perhaps she will listen to you." Lady Hartshore smiled, but her expression was far from convinced. They both knew the flamboyant cook rarely accepted advice from anyone. If she desired to threaten a guest in the house with her cleaver, that was precisely what she would do.

"I should be on my way," Cedric murmured, realizing he had accomplished all he could for the moment.

"You will not stay for luncheon?" his aunt demanded in obvious disappointment.

"No, I must see to the thatching on old Peter's cottage. But I do hope that you and Miss Cresswell will agree to join me for luncheon tomorrow at Hartshore Park."

Cassie clapped her hands together. "What a lovely notion. We would be delighted, would we not, Miss Cresswell?"

Cedric turned to catch the ripple of dismay that crossed Miss Cresswell's delicate features before it was sternly dismissed.

"Delighted," she said in bland tones.

With a decidedly mocking smile he offered her an elegant bow.

"Until tomorrow, my dear."

Six

Stepping into the vaulted foyer of Hartshore Park, Emma attempted to still the peculiar flutters in the pit of her stomach.

She was a fool to have come.

Why hadn't she feigned some illness? A headache. A sudden chill. A brain fever. Leprosy.

Anything to keep her safely in the privacy of her chamber.

Because that dratted Lord Hartshore would have instantly known the truth, a small voice answered in the back of her mind. He would have known she was being a coward. And that was something she couldn't bear.

Why could he not be like other gentlemen? she seethed.

She was accustomed to polite indifference, cool dismissal, or even the cut direct. She was unprepared for his determined effort to ruffle her hard-won composure.

How did a lady ignore a gentleman who defied all normal conventions?

He laughed at her impervious demeanor, mocked her desire to be treated as a servant, deliberately stirred the embers of her anger, and caressed her without warning. Good heavens, he kissed her without warning.

It was utterly frustrating.

And yet . . .

And yet, when she had gone to sleep last night, it had been with a pink rose on her pillow.

Emma gave a sharp shake of her head.

Clearly, her short time in Kent had already addled her once nicely predictable wits. The sooner she returned to London, the better.

Stepping into the foyer, the butler performed a dignified bow.

"Welcome, Lady Hartshore," he murmured.

"Winters." Lady Hartshore smiled warmly at the elderly servant. "How well you are looking."

There was a faint softening of the dignified expression. "Thank you, my lady."

"I hope your family is in good health?"

"Quite good," he assured her, then waved an arm toward the staircase. "Lord Hartshore is in the library."

"We will show ourselves in."

"Very good." With another bow the butler silently disappeared into the shadows.

Emma took a step toward the stairs, only to be halted as Lady Hartshore laid a hand on her arm.

"Oh, I have just recalled, I must have a word with Mrs. Freeman," she stated in firm tones. "The library is the first door on the right, my dear."

Emma's eyes widened with dismay. She had no need for directions. For goodness' sake, she had been carried to the room in the arms of Lord Hartshore mere days ago. She could no doubt find it with her eyes closed. She had no desire, however, to arrive without the presence of Lady Hartshore.

"Oh, but . . ."

Unfortunately the older woman did not remain to hear her protests as she bustled down the hall with determined steps.

Drat.

How did she keep being forced into situations where she was alone with Lord Hartshore?

Not even engaged maidens were allowed to spend such time alone with their fiancés.

With decidedly reluctant steps she climbed the sweeping stairs. She even halted on several occasions to study the framed oil paintings that lined the paneled walls.

Not a difficult task, she acknowledged as she peered at a stunning Raphael. Trained by her father, she could easily discern that it was a true masterpiece. The colors were vibrant and the strokes possessed a bold genius.

With a tiny sigh of appreciation Emma forced herself to continue up the steps and toward the open door of the library.

She could delay the inevitable no longer, she acknowledged. Lord Hartshore had no doubt already heard her hesitant steps and was wondering what the devil could take so long to traverse such a short distance.

As if to prove her point, Lord Hartshore abruptly stepped into the hallway, bringing with him a powerful force that filled the very air.

Sunlight filtered from the library to slant across his dark features and shimmered in his golden eyes. His broad frame was outlined with faithful precision in a sapphire-blue coat and buff breeches. And, as always, a smile that could melt the most frigid heart curved his lips.

Really, she silently told herself, that smile was beyond the bounds of decency. No gentleman should be allowed to trot about, flashing it indiscriminately at unsuspecting females.

Perhaps sensing her dark thoughts, Lord Hartshore allowed that bothersome smile to widen.

"Welcome to my home, Miss Cresswell," he said in smoky tones.

Quite without warning Emma felt the palms of her hands begin to sweat.

It was the most peculiar thing.

"Lady Hartshore is with Mrs. Freeman," she said abruptly, as much to remind herself her time alone with this gentleman would be short-lived as to explain the woman's absence to Lord Hartshore.

"Good," he said firmly.

"Excuse me?"

"This gives me the perfect opportunity to show you my home." He held out his arm in invitation. "Shall we?"

There were no doubt a dozen perfectly legitimate reasons for her to decline his invitation. Unfortunately at the moment Emma could not think of a single one.

Cursing Lady Hartshore for abandoning her, Emma stiffly moved forward to place her hand on his arm.

"Where are we going?" she asked as he led her down the long corridor.

The golden eyes held a distinct twinkle as he glanced down at her set features.

"To my very favorite room, Miss Cresswell."

She did not doubt that he intended to bring a blush to her cheeks, and she hastily averted her face to study the pretty pier tables and satinwood chairs that lined the hall.

A faint chuckle echoed through the air, but thankfully he remained silent as they turned a corner and headed down a narrow set of stairs.

Emma had lost all sense of direction as they traveled down one hall and then another until at last he pushed open a door to reveal a vast iron-and-glass conservatory.

She felt her breath catch at the beautiful flowers that were banked along the marble pathway. At the far end, a pretty fountain sparkled in the sunlight surrounded by wrought-iron benches that beckoned one to be seated and simply appreciate the beauty of nature.

"Oh," she breathed, fully appreciating the warm, musky scent of earth and roses.

"Come," he urged softly, leading her down the narrow path. "These are my English varieties," he explained as he pointed to the closest rose plants. "On the other side are the ones that I purchased in China, and farther along are those I have selected from Europe."

Emma gave a faint shake of her head. "It is amazing."

They continued toward the fountain, then Lord Hartshore halted beside a separate bank of blooming roses. Emma recognized the wood nymph the moment her gaze caught sight of the dusky pink buds, and her heart gave an odd twitch.

"These are the roses that I am crossbreeding," he said with a hint of satisfaction.

"Do you care for all of these?" she demanded in disbelief.

"With the help of my gardeners."

Briefly forgetting just how unnerving she found this man, she glanced up to meet his watchful gaze.

"Why roses?"

"I find them fascinating," he admitted without apology. "Did you know that both the Greeks and Romans used roses in their festivals? And the Egyptians called a particular bloom the Holy Rose?"

"No."

"And, of course, there is the long-held belief that the essence of the rose is medicinal as well as beautiful."

"It is rather an unusual occupation."

"Not that unusual," he denied. "It is said that Josephine is a keen rose-breeder and that she has collected dozens of varieties at her Palace of Malmaison." Abruptly leaning forward, he plucked one of the pink blooms and pressed it into her hand. "For you."

"Will you truly call it wood nymph?"

"I can think of no more perfect name," he said, reaching out to stroke a velvet petal. "Like any good wood nymph, it is beautiful in an unassuming manner, it has an enchanting allure, and while it is fragile to the touch, it possesses sharp thorns for the unwary."

Her lips gave a reneged twitch at his audacious words. "Very poetic."

"I have my moments," he murmured.

Oh, yes, he certainly had his moments, she acknowledged with a small shiver.

Dangerous moments . . . when he seemed able to make the very air crackle about her.

"Perhaps we should return to Lady Hartshore," she said in oddly breathless tones.

"I am certain my aunt is happily chatting with the servants. This was her home while married to my uncle, and she hired much of the staff. She considers them all a part of her family."

Emma did not doubt his words. Lady Hartshore had already proven to be a countess without pretensions. There was no one she did not halt to converse with, including servants, tenants, and, on unnerving occasions, her dead husband.

"I still think it best to return and await her."

With a bold disregard for propriety he lifted his hands to trace the line of her shoulders.

"There is no hurry."

She sucked in a shaky breath, willing herself not to become lost in the golden warmth of his eyes.

"My lord."

"I like seeing you among my roses," he said as he stepped close enough to bathe her in the heat of his body. "Such a combination of beauty is quite heady."

"What are you doing?"

He smiled as one hand moved to cup the back of her neck. "I am going to kiss you, Miss Cresswell."

She shivered as a delicious tension clutched at her stomach.

"Now?" she absurdly blurted out.

"Yes, now," he whispered, lowering his head to claim her lips in a kiss that sent a shock of poignant sweetness to the very tips of her curled toes.

Emma knew she should protest.

It was utterly improper to be kissing the nephew of her employer. Especially a nephew who had been a wretched nuisance since she first encountered him.

But the hands that rose to push him away instead smoothed over the chiseled muscles of his chest.

Her lashes fluttered downward as his free arm wrapped around her waist. With a slow insistence the kiss deepened, making Emma tremble with a building excitement.

Magic.

That was how Lord Hartshore described this fierce awareness that jolted to life when they were near each other.

And just for the moment Emma was willing to believe him.

What other explanation could there be for the manner her heart thundered in her chest? And how her body willingly arched toward the hardness of his frame?

She felt his tongue gently trace the outline of her trembling lips before he pulled back to gaze at her flushed face.

"What are you doing to me, Miss Cresswell?" he murmured in a husky voice. "You are a distraction I had not anticipated."

A shiver raced down her spine at the hunger that abruptly blazed in the golden eyes.

"We should not be doing this," she whispered in uneven tones.

A sudden hint of amusement softened the male features. "Quite possibly not."

"My lord." With an effort she forced her hands to push at the hard strength of his chest.

For a moment he gazed down into her wide eyes, and Emma trembled with the effort to not sway forward. A traitorous part of her longed for him to ignore her protest. To simply sweep her back against him and to drown all common sense in the heat of his kisses. Slowly his gaze lowered to her parted lips, and Emma caught her breath as she waited for his dark head to swoop downward.

But instead, he heaved a rueful sigh and with obvious reluctance allowed his hands to drop.

"Very well. As much as I would prefer to linger, I suppose we should return to the library."

The sharp pang of regret was sternly smothered as Emma ran shaking hands over the folds of her skirt. Dear heavens, she could not be disappointed that she wasn't about to be seduced in the rose-scented conservatory, could she?

No, of course not, she chastised her foolishness.

Lord Hartshore was a handsome, extraordinarily charming gentleman who was clearly a master at pleasing a woman. While she . . . well, there was no denying that she was more innocent than most schoolgirls.

It was little wonder she had been briefly carried away.

The danger lay in presuming it was anything more than a passing incident that should be dismissed from her mind with all possible speed.

"Yes," Emma said firmly, hoping she did not appear as flustered as she felt.

With a brisk movement she turned around to head back up the pathway. She would not press a hand to her tingling lips, she told herself over and over. She would not give him the satisfaction of knowing she felt thoroughly and satisfyingly kissed.

Intent on maintaining a cool demeanor, Emma barely noted the faint sounds of scratching that could be heard in the distance. It was not until a small, tawny ball of fluff hurtled through the doorway that she realized the sound came from puppy paws upon the slick marble. All sense of tension fled from her as the puppy attempted to halt its headlong flight, only to awkwardly slide into her skirts.

Bending downward, she freed the struggling puppy from her skirts, giving an unconscious laugh as the dog promptly rewarded her efforts by placing its paws upon her knees and lavishing her face with wet kisses.

"Pudge, down," Lord Hartshore commanded in firm tones, only to sigh in fond exasperation as the puppy blithely ignored him. "You must forgive the scoundrel, Miss Cresswell. His manners are deplorable and he is hopelessly spoiled."

She lifted her head to meet his amused gaze. "Pudge?"

"Well, his true name is Hannibal, but he is far too lazy and fat for a great commander, so he has become Pudge," he explained, an odd stillness settling around him as he studied her unguarded expression. "I fear that he is as fond of kisses as myself."

Her heart gave a far too pleasurable flop, and she ducked her head back toward Pudge. Puppy kisses were infinitely less dangerous than those of a rogue.

"I do not mind," she murmured.

"Do you know," he said in low tones, "that this is the first time I have ever seen you genuinely smile?"

She refused to glance up, afraid of becoming lost in that compelling golden gaze.

"I like dogs."

"Egads, a killing thrust, Miss Cresswell," he retorted at her unwitting words. "Shall we return to the library before my pride is fatally wounded?"

It was with a great deal of stealth that Cedric managed to enter Mayford the following afternoon without being detected. Although he supposed it was not precisely proper to be seeking out Miss Cresswell when he knew his aunt would be in her chambers resting, it did not halt him from slipping through a side entrance and toward the back parlor, where he expected to find the young maiden.

He had not lied when he said he cared very little for propriety. To his mind, it was all a great deal of nonsense. What did it matter if a person looked and pretended to be all that was respectable when their heart was as black as sin? Besides, among Society, propriety meant only that one wasn't supposed to get caught being improper.

He intended no harm to Miss Cresswell. He wished only to speak with her without the kindly but inquisitive interest of his aunt.

A tiny smile curved his lips as he recalled their last occasion alone.

Good Lord, he had told himself that nothing could compare to the fierce pleasure he had experienced during their first kiss. After all, the first kiss with any woman was always special. But the moment their lips had met, he realized his mistake. The same consuming heat had flooded through his body, combined with the strangest flare of tenderness that had tugged at his heart.

He wanted to lay her onto the moist soil and plunder her innocence at the same moment he wanted to sweep her in his arms and protect her from the world.

It was all vastly confusing.

And not only for himself.

He was well aware that after a few days to ponder what had occurred between them, Miss Cresswell would have possessed ample opportunity to deeply regret her momentary weakness. He wanted to ensure that she did not manage to create an impenetrable barrier between them.

And he had brought with him the perfect weapon, he told himself, halting beside the door to lay down his bundle.

Pausing to adjust his coat, Cedric pushed open the door and stepped into the long room. As he suspected, Miss Cresswell was seated near the fire, stitching upon a piece of linen. At his entrance, however, she jerkily rose to her feet and regarded him in a wary fashion.

"My lord."

"Miss Cresswell." He offered a bow.

"I fear your aunt has gone to her chambers. I will let her know that you have called."

He held up a hand as she prepared to flee, no doubt intending to disappear to her own chambers the moment she was out of sight.

"Actually, I have come to see you, and I have brought you a visitor."

A frown marred her wide brow, but at his low whistle her eyes widened in sudden pleasure.

"Pudge." She readily lowered herself as the puppy scrambled into the room and promptly raced to her feet.

Ruefully smiling at the knowledge that the dog had proved to be a more effective enticement than his own charms, Cedric stepped farther into the room.

"I hoped you would be pleased. We have been working very hard these past few days."

She reluctantly straightened to meet his smile. "Oh?"

"Yes, and Pudge wished to show you how very clever he has become."

"I see."

Assuming a stern manner, he moved to steer her into the center of the room. He considered it a decided miracle when she did not instantly cringe from his touch.

"Stand here," he ordered, then, turning to the puppy, he snapped his fingers. "Sit, Pudge, sit."

Wagging his tail the dog promptly barked at Cedric with unbridled enthusiasm.

At his side he heard the minx choke back a laugh. "Very clever," she commended.

Flashing her a mock frown, Cedric once again snapped his fingers.

"Speak, Pudge." On cue the dog abruptly rolled onto his back, waving his stubby legs in the air. There was another choked laugh at his side. "Pudge, play dead," he ordered.

Rising back to his feet, Pudge determinedly scratched at one ear, then suddenly noticing the tail out of the corner of his eye, he set about chasing the new toy with abandoned joy. Turning his head, Cedric caught the distinct twinkle in the emerald eyes.

"Astonishing," she murmured. "You might consider joining a circus."

"Bad dog," Cedric chided the puppy, only to laugh as Pudge happily danced to his feet and laid his paws upon his gleaming boots. Reaching into his pocket he produced a scrap of bacon. "Here you go, you treacherous beast."

Watching their antics, Miss Cresswell gave a slow shake of her head.

"I am not entirely certain who has trained whom."

Wiping his fingers on a handkerchief, Cedric turned so that he could give his undivided attention to her beautiful countenance.

"Well, he did accomplish what I most desired."

"And what is that?"

"He conjured that most elusive smile," he said softly.

A hint of color filled her cheeks as she took a hasty step backward.

"Did you wish to leave a message for Lady Hartshore?"

Although Cedric regretted the loss of her unfettered enjoyment, he was content that she had not resumed the chilly distance she had bestowed upon him when he had first entered the room.

"No, I merely wished to see how you were settling in."

"Well enough, thank you."

"I trust that your duties are not overly burdensome?"

Her expression became wry at his probing. "As I'm sure you must have deduced, I have no duties."

He shrugged. "You are giving an elderly woman comfort and companionship. What other duties do you need?"

"I like to feel useful," she retorted, her hands absently plucking at the thick gray material of her skirt.

Cedric gave a slow shake of his head. What other maiden would not be delighted to discover her role as a servant was instead one as a guest?

"Perhaps you are more useful than you suspect," he suggested.

She opened her mouth to deny his words, but before she could utter a sound, the door to the parlor was thrust open and the wide form of Mrs. Borelli entered the room. With a sly glance in Cedric's direction, she moved to place a heavy tray laden with tea and cakes upon a table.

"I thought you might be in here, my lord," she said in suggestive tones. "I brought you nice hot tea and your favorite scones."

Rather surprised at having being so easily caught out, Cedric flashed her a boyish grin.

"You are a jewel among cooks, Mrs. Borelli."

She snorted at his obvious flattery, then leaned forward to peer at him with obvious interest.

"Come by for a reading afore you leave. I sense a change in the air."

"A change?" Cedric teasingly arched his brows. "That sounds fascinating."

"Fah," Miss Cresswell abruptly muttered beneath her breath.

Cedric gave a chiding click of his tongue. "I fear we have a disbeliever among us, Mrs. Borelli."

"Ah." With movements that were surprisingly swift in such a large lady, the cook had reached out to grasp Miss Cresswell's unsuspecting hand. "Let me have a look."

"No." The young lady attempted to pull free her hand. "I do not think . . ."

"I see a man," Mrs. Borelli droned, ignoring the girl's attempt to wrench her hand away. "Tall, with dark hair."

Cedric's smile widened. Mrs. Borelli was harmless despite her firm belief in reading the future. "Is he handsome?"

"Of course." The cook continued to study the lines upon Miss Cresswell's palm. "And children. Many children. Three girls and three boys."

"Nonsense," Miss Cresswell breathed.

Cedric gave a sharp laugh at the embarrassment staining her cheeks. "Anything else?"

"Happiness," Mrs. Borelli finished simply.

"A most delightful future," he complimented the disbelieving Miss Cresswell.

He was rewarded with a scowl. "I am glad you find this amusing."

The cook silenced them with a purse of her lips. "I have not yet read the past," she declared, once again pondering the upturned palm. "I see three girls. Sisters . . . very close. And a man. He is hard to read, but he has caused you great pain."

Cedric's smile faded as he watched the color abruptly drain from Miss Cresswell's tiny face.

"That is enough," she rasped, angrily pulling her hand free.

Undaunted, the cook reached out to lightly touch the emerald hung around the maiden's neck.

"It has to do with this. It ties you to the past."

Realizing that somehow Mrs. Borelli had managed to strike a painful nerve within Miss Cresswell, Cedric stepped forward to place a protective arm around her shoulders.

"I believe Miss Cresswell has become convinced."

The older woman leaned forward. "You must heal your heart before you can love again," she said mysteriously before giving a nod of her head and turning to leave the room.

Realizing that the slender form was trembling beneath his arm, Cedric slowly led her to the sofa and settled her upon the cushion. Then, taking a seat next to her, he quickly poured a cup of the steaming tea and added a goodly measure of sugar.

"Here." He firmly pressed the cup into her hands and watched as she absently took a drink. "I am sorry if Mrs. Borelli upset you. She truly does believe she can see the future and the past."

A shudder shook her body, but with an obvious effort she attempted to hide the shock that had left her pale and shaken.

"She did not upset me," she ridiculously lied. "It is all a great deal of nonsense."

"If you say," he murmured soothingly.

Glancing down at the fingers that clenched the cup so tightly he feared it might shatter, Cedric silently promised himself that he would discover what it was that she kept locked so deeply inside her.

And then . . .

In truth, he did not know what he would do then.

He knew only that he wanted to see the shadows erased from those emerald eyes and a smile upon those enchanting lips.

Only then would he be satisfied.

Seven

During the course of the next two days, Emma managed to convince herself that she had been a thorough ninny to be disturbed by Mrs. Borelli's ridiculous fortune-telling.

After all, what had she said that was so startling?

Three sisters?

No doubt the cook had overheard her speak of Sarah and Rachel.

And as for a man who had caused her pain . . . well, Mrs. Borelli would not be the first to presume Emma's brilliant emerald pendant had been a gift from a lover who had tossed her aside.

Besides, she had only to remind herself of the woman's absurd claim that she would wed a handsome gentleman and produce six children to prove to herself the nonsense of the entire incident.

The only thing remarkable about the fortune-telling was that she had even momentarily allowed it to rattle her.

Seated upon the window seat of the back parlor, Emma attempted to concentrate on the pretty floral design she had stamped upon the white linen. Lady Hartshore had disappeared to her chambers nearly an hour before, and as occurred far too often, Emma discovered herself with time on her hands.

She was unaccustomed to lazy afternoons with nothing more pressing than enjoying tea and reminding Lady Hartshore when it was time to change for dinner. She preferred to be busy so that she did not have the opportunity to brood upon ridiculous fortune-tellers, the kisses of charming rogues, and the undoubted pleasure of being treated as an honored guest rather than as a despised servant.

Such thoughts were far too dangerous.

Swallowing a sigh, Emma tossed aside her needlework and rose to her feet. She was feeling far too restless for such a placid pastime. What she needed was a brisk walk to clear her thoughts, she decided. She had discovered that there was something quite refreshing about strolling through the countryside despite the chill January wind. She could even chuckle over her initial fear of bandits and evil cows. Now when she stepped outside she was only aware of the quiet grandeur that surrounded her.

Moving across the room so that she could collect her spencer, Emma abruptly halted as the door was thrown open and Lady Hartshore hurried in with a wide smile.

"Valentine's Day," the older woman pronounced in expectant tones.

Emma gave a startled blink. "Pardon me?"

"Fredrick just reminded me that it will soon be Valentine's Day."

"Oh, yes, I suppose it will be," Emma murmured, barely noting she was agreeing with the long-departed Lord Hartshore.

"You know, since Fredrick's death I have done little to celebrate the day, since, of course, my true love has passed to the other side," Lady Hartshore chattered as she moved to perch on the edge of a delicately scrolled sofa. "But while he was alive we always hosted the most marvelous balls."

Realizing that her employer was in the mood to recall

the happy days of her past, Emma obligingly resumed her place on the window seat. It was the only duty she was allowed to perform.

"That must have been lovely," she said with an encouraging smile.

"Oh, they were so charming." Lady Hartshore leaned forward, eagerly recalling her triumph as a hostess. "You see, it was always a masquerade ball. The guests would disguise themselves as famous lovers. You know, Romeo and Juliet, Casanova, Adam and Eve. One year Fredrick and I went as Samson and Delilah. I had the loveliest gown, although it was a trifle scandalous. And at midnight we would reveal our true identities. It was all very romantic, and you would be surprised to know how many young maidens became engaged after being swept off their feet by a masked lover."

Having been to more than one ball, Emma was aware most maidens were embarrassingly eager to be swept off their feet. Indeed, a few of the more bold damsels were not so much swept as they were caught as they tossed themselves headlong at an unsuspecting gentleman.

"Did they?"

"Oh, yes, Miss Satter, who wed Lord Josten, and both the Miller twins, who married brothers, if you can believe, and Miss Foster, who captured the most elusive Colonel Daggs. And Lady Ellison . . . now, whom did she wed? Crest? Cross?" Lady Hartshore gave a faint shrug. "Well, no matter, they have all been the happiest connections. Do you suppose it is because they fell in love on Valentine's Day?"

"I'm sure I couldn't say," Emma had to admit.

Lady Hartshore heaved a happy sigh. "Such a grand evening. Music and dancing and Valentine cards and stolen kisses in the corner." Her words came to a sudden halt as she suddenly straightened. "You know, Miss Cresswell . . ."

"Yes?"

"There is no reason we shouldn't host a ball."

Emma felt a flare of panic. Although there was little chance that anyone within the neighborhood would recognize her as the daughter of the Devilish Dandy, she had no desire to take the risk. Besides, she possessed an unshakable dislike for such frivolous entertainment. She had painfully learned that they were little more than a ready-made opportunity to spread vicious gossip and rip reputations to shreds.

"On Valentine's Day?" she demanded, hoping that the older woman would admit there would not be adequate time to prepare such a lavish event.

"Of course." Lady Hartshore was swift to confirm the worst. "It has been too long since I have entertained."

Emma clenched her hands in her lap. Trust her to be around the moment Lady Hartshore plunged back into the social whirl.

"I thought you preferred to live quietly?" she reminded the older woman.

"One ball is not precisely a life of debauchery," Lady Hartshore said in gentle tones.

"No," Emma acknowledged with a prick of guilt at attempting to dampen the woman's obvious enthusiasm. It had obviously been years since Lady Hartshore had felt the desire to entertain. Only the most selfish beast would seek to discourage her. "I suppose not."

The pleased smile returned. "It will be delightful, you will see. But there is so much to be done in a very short period of time. First we must concentrate on the invitations. Do you not think it would be clever to do them as Valentine cards?"

Emma could only hope that her expression did not appear as stiff as it felt.

"Yes."

With a swift motion Lady Hartshore was on her feet, her hands pressed together.

"I shall begin making out the list this moment."

She scurried from the room, leaving behind a bemused Emma.

Well, if she hadn't needed a brisk walk before, she certainly needed one now, Emma told herself wryly.

With determined steps she moved out of the room, then, collecting her spencer, she headed for the solitude of the garden.

Once assured she was alone, she slowed her steps and drew in a deep breath.

A Valentine ball?

The mere thought was enough to give her the hives.

Hardly surprising, she admitted.

The last ball she had attended had been an unmitigated disaster.

Her eyes grew dark as she recalled the horrid night. Strangely, it had all started off so well. Sarah had ordered her a new gown with white lace and tiny roses around the hem. She had been surrounded by eager young gentlemen the moment she had entered the ballroom, making her feel almost beautiful.

Unfortunately she had not realized that her father had been captured that morning, nor that his true identity was spreading through London with the speed of a wildfire. It was not until the hostess had approached her in the middle of the dance floor and shrilly demanded that she leave her house at once that she understood what had occurred.

Emma would never forget the long walk from the silent room. Or the disgusted gazes from her supposed friends as she had left.

Not one soul stepped forward to ease the shame that clutched at her heart. Or offered her a kind word to prove their loyalty.

She had been condemned a social outcast and no one would risk her bitter plight. Reputation was of far greater importance than loyalty or friendship to those of the *ton*.

Less than two weeks later, Emma had taken a position as governess for the Falwells.

Emma gave a faint shake of her head.

She supposed she had always known that the truth of her father would be revealed. Perhaps even a part of her had accepted the humiliating episode as her due for being the daughter of the Devilish Dandy. But that did not ease the regret that still lingered deep in her heart.

How different might her life have been had she been just ordinary Miss Cresswell and not the notorious daughter of the Devilish Dandy, she thought.

Would she be wed with her own family?

Would she be surrounded by friends?

"Miss Crane."

Pulled out of her thoughts by the imperious call, Emma reluctantly turned to discover Mr. Allensway hurrying in her direction. Her heart sank at the sight of his determined expression.

"Oh, Miss Crane," he called again, as if fearing she might make a mad dash for freedom before he could catch her.

Not that the thought did not cross her mind, she acknowledged as the gentleman came to a halt beside her. There was something in the vicar's thin smile that sent a rash of warning through her.

"Cresswell," she corrected him in firm tones.

He regarded her in puzzlement. "Pardon me?"

"My name is Miss Cresswell."

"Ah . . . yes." He gave a shrug, as if the name of a mere servant were irrelevant. "May I have a moment?"

"If you wish."

As if sensing her reluctance, Mr. Allensway stretched his smile to reveal his prominent teeth.

"How are you enjoying Kent?"

She eyed him warily, well aware he had not approached her to discuss her opinion of Kent.

"It is very peaceful."

"Yes." He fingered his stiff cravat. "Tell me, did you know Lady Hartshore before becoming her companion?"

"No, I was hired in London."

"Ah." He gave a delicate cough. "Then it must have been something of a shock when you arrived at Mayford."

Emma hid a wry smile. Shock was rather an understatement.

"It was not precisely what I had been expecting," she hedged.

The vicar gave a sympathetic click of his tongue. "No, a gently reared lady such as yourself must find it very awkward. Yes, very awkward."

Oddly, Emma stiffened at his soft words. He was saying nothing more than she had said to herself on a dozen separate occasions. And yet she could not deny the stab of anger that raced through her body.

"Lady Hartshore is very kind."

"Oh, yes, do not think that I do not greatly admire Lady Hartshore. And, of course, Mr. Carson," he smoothly assured her, pressing his hands to his heart in a futile effort to appear sincere. "Still, I do find myself concerned at your unfortunate position."

Her eyes narrowed. "Unfortunate position?"

"Well, my dear, you must realize that this rather peculiar household is bound to cause its share of gossip. I would not like to see an innocent maiden's reputation tarnished in any manner."

She should have trembled with fear at his words. His insinuations struck at her deepest concerns. How could she bear to once again be the center of gossip and cruel amusement?

Instead, her hands clenched in anger.

"I have done nothing to tarnish my reputation, Mr. Allensway."

The gentleman sent her a pitying glance. "Simply being at Mayford is enough to set tongues wagging, I fear. You know how people can be. And Lady Hartshore's odd behavior is bound to create twitters."

"I would hope that true Christians would have more productive things to do with their time than mock others," she said in cold tones.

Undaunted, Mr. Allensway lifted his hands in a helpless motion. "Indeed, but human nature is human nature."

Emma had endured enough. She was well acquainted with human nature. Including bumptious encroachers who cared for nothing beyond their selfish desires.

Commanding an unconscious hauteur, she glared at her unwelcome companion in an icy fashion.

"What do you desire from me, Mr. Allensway?"

The vicar appeared momentarily startled by her less than servile demeanor. Then, with an ingratiating smile, he at last came to the point of his visit.

"Well, as you are in a position of trust with Lady Hartshore, I thought perhaps you might speak with her concerning her habit of referring to Lord Hartshore as if he were still alive. I'm certain that a few well-spoken words would reveal to her that such ungodly behavior is unseemly for a countess."

So, that was why he had lowered himself to speak with a mere servant, she thought with a flare of disgust. The nasty little toad.

"Lady Hartshore truly believes that she speaks with her husband. No one can convince her otherwise," she said in lofty tones.

His lips thinned at her perverse refusal to concede to his wishes.

"At least you could speak to her about the gossip she is stirring. It does, after all, affect you as well."

At the moment Emma had no thought to the inevitable gossip that might be twittering through the neighborhood. She knew only that Lady Hartshore was a kind and generous woman who was far superior to this nodcock.

"No, Mr. Allensway."

He gave a blink of surprise. "What?"

"No, I will not speak with Lady Hartshore regarding her husband," she said in slow, concise tones. "Not only is it not my place, but I have no desire to do so. If it comforts her to speak with Lord Hartshore, then it is no one else's concern. Least of all yours."

Without warning the sound of clapping hands rang through the garden and the large form of Lord Hartshore stepped from behind a hedge.

"Bravo, Miss Cresswell," he congratulated Emma, smiling deep into her startled eyes.

Cedric was not above eavesdropping.

When he had spotted Miss Cresswell and the vicar in the garden, he had deliberately moved to stand behind the hedge.

He had no interest in Mr. Allensway. There was no doubt the sly little twit was up to something devious. He would never lower himself to speak with a mere servant unless he hoped to gain something from the situation. But he was very curious in how Miss Cresswell would respond to the vicar's demands.

He had not been disappointed.

She had not even paused in her staunch defense of her employer. Despite her own misgivings and reluctance to remain at Mayford, she had protected Lady Hartshore with a fierce loyalty that had made his heart flare with warmth.

Miss Cresswell might profess a burning desire to return to London, but she was no more immune to the charm of Lady Hartshore than anyone else.

All except the local vicar.

Slowly turning from the lovely countenance of Miss Cresswell, he stabbed Mr. Allensway with a glittering gaze.

"Mr. Allensway."

Clearly uneasy at being caught in his attempt to recruit Miss Cresswell, the gentleman gave a hasty bow.

"My lord. A fine day, is it not?"

"It was," Cedric deliberately drawled. "Why are you here?"

A dark flush stained the vicar's countenance. "I merely wished to visit with Miss Cresswell."

"Really?" He folded his arms over the width of his chest. "Surely a vicar has more pressing duties than pestering my aunt's companion?"

"Of course." His smile was sickly as he performed another bow. "Good day."

With satisfying haste the vicar scurried from the garden and with a rueful shake of his head Cedric turned back to Miss Cresswell. She was busily frowning at the retreating Mr. Allensway, and Cedric allowed himself a moment to sigh over her serviceable dark spencer that covered an even more serviceable gray gown.

Just once he wished to see her attired in a dress that was not utterly repulsive. Perhaps a deep blue silk, or ivory satin with Brussels lace. Or even a pale rose gauze with a neckline . . .

He abruptly brought a halt to his train of thought as he realized that his imaginary gowns were becoming more sheer and revealing with every passing moment.

Good heavens, he was close to having her stripped naked.

Not that he wouldn't enjoy stripping her naked, a treacherous voice whispered. He had no doubt that beneath those layers of hideous gray was a body that would inflame any gentleman.

"I am sorry that Mr. Allensway bothered you," he forced himself to say before he could no longer hide the direction of his scandalous thoughts.

Her frown abruptly lifted as she turned to meet his deliberately bland expression.

"He is very persistent."

"That is a polite manner of describing him," he said wryly. "Still, I have no desire to mar this lovely day with thoughts of Mr. Allensway. I brought you this."

He watched in pleasure as a blush touched her cheeks, and she reached out to take the rose he had plucked before leaving Hartshore Park.

"Thank you." A bewitching confusion rippled over her features before she restored the polite mask. "Did you wish to see your aunt?"

"Perhaps later. For now I have something I wish to show you."

"What is it?"

He flashed her a devilish smile. "It is a surprise."

"Another surprise?"

"Oh, I am filled with surprises," he assured her.

Her brows lifted. "So I am beginning to realize."

"Shall we?"

He held out his arm, and after only a moment's pause she placed her gloved hand upon his sleeve. Cedric hid his sense of triumph as he led her through the garden and toward the surrounding parkland. He had half expected to have to toss the contrary chit over his shoulder to convince her to accompany him. He could only suppose that she was too overset by her confrontation with Mr. Allensway to recall that she disliked his company.

"Is it far?" she at last demanded as they angled toward the copse of trees that marched beside Hartshore Park.

"No, not far. Of course, you must tell me if you are cold. I would not wish you to become ill."

"My constitution is quite hardy."

"So you are not one of those females who find pleasure in always being frail?" he teased.

She wrinkled her nose in distaste. "I have little patience with such foolishness. My last employer was quite dedicated to presuming herself stricken with one illness or another. She spent entire months laying abed with no company beyond her doctor."

"And no doubt expecting you to fetch and carry for her night and day," he surmised.

She gave a shrug. "At times."

"It sounds as if you are well rid of her."

"Yes, I suppose," she slowly agreed.

His frown abruptly lifted as he easily read her thoughts. "Even if it did land you in Bedlam."

A renegade smile twitched at her full lips. "Yes."

"We at least do not make you fetch and carry. And for the most part we are a harmless lot."

The emerald gaze suddenly lifted to meet his steady regard. "I am not entirely certain I would consider you harmless, my lord."

He gave a short laugh. "Perhaps not. I do possess a most violent fascination for wood nymphs."

Her head ducked at his teasing, but he had no doubt that a delightful color was staining her cheeks. A strange sense of contentment settled in the region of his heart as he pulled her even closer and entered the fringe of trees. He had exchanged such banter with dozens of women. Some sophisticated, some coy, and some far more experienced than himself. But none of them had managed to stir more than a fleeting desire. He was uncertain why this particular woman managed to strike so much deeper.

The sound of chattering voices echoed through the chilled air, and with a frown of puzzlement Miss Cresswell lifted her head.

"Who is that?"

"A traveling theater group," he explained as they entered a small clearing to reveal a dozen mingling actors attired in brilliant if rather battered clothing. "They are on their way to Canterbury and requested to use the clearing to rehearse. I thought you might wish to watch."

The ripple of pleasure that crossed her countenance was all that he wished for as she nodded her head.

"Yes."

Spotting their arrival, a thin gentleman dressed in a gaudy crimson coat and cape detached himself from the group and hurried to greet them with a flamboyant bow.

"My lord, such an honor to welcome you."

"This is Miss Cresswell." Cedric indicated his companion. "Miss Cresswell, Gaston, the manager of the troupe."

"Mr. Gaston."

The manager waved his hands in a Gallic fashion. "No, no. Merely Gaston. Now I must tend to business. Please enjoy."

He bolted away as swiftly as he had arrived, and realizing he was calling the actors to take their places, Cedric led Miss Cresswell to a rough bench that had been situated close to a large covered-wagon.

"Cold?" he asked as he settled close to her slender form.

"Not at all," she assured him, her gaze never leaving the makeshift stage that was swiftly being assembled.

Ruefully acknowledging that he had been thoroughly dismissed from Miss Cresswell's thoughts, Cedric made himself as comfortable as possible and turned his own attention to the actors. Within moments they were prepared.

Although it was far from a polished rendition of *The Country Wife,* and the leading man had a tendency to mug and upstage the remaining cast, there was enough ridiculous humor to make the performance bearable. Most enjoyable, however, was watching the rigid control that Miss Cresswell shrouded around herself slowly disappear. There was even a smile upon her face by the time the actors took their bows. This was how he wished her always to be, he thought with an inner sigh. Unfettered by the shadows that dimmed her natural spirit.

Pressing himself to his feet, Cedric helped Miss Cresswell to rise as Gaston hurried in their direction along with a tall, overly handsome leading man and a lush raven-haired actress with an inviting smile.

"My lord, Miss Cresswell." Gaston waved his hands toward his two companions. "May I introduce Raymond Field and Anna Fray?"

Cedric barely noted the lovely actress who attached herself to his arm and offered her conveniently exposed charms for his inspection. Instead, his attention was trained on the oily-smooth gentleman who had brazenly claimed Miss Cresswell's hand and raised it to his lips.

"Miss Cresswell, what a charming surprise," he murmured in rich tones. "Did you enjoy the performance?"

Shockingly, the perverse minx offered him a ready smile. Far more readily than she had ever offered one to him, Cedric acknowledged with a hint of annoyance.

"Very much."

"It is a bit rough, but all will come together before we reach Canterbury." The bounder continued his hold on Miss Cresswell's fingers, unaware how close he was to having his perfect Grecian nose broken. "It always does."

"It must be difficult to travel so much."

"Oh, I don't know." He leaned forward. "I get to meet many fascinating people."

The beautiful Anna tugged on his coat, obviously wishing to gain his attention, but Cedric refused to shift his gaze from Miss Cresswell's delicate profile.

"Yes, I suppose you do," she said softly.

The actor squeezed her fingers. "Some more fascinating than others."

Enough was enough.

Firmly shaking off the clinging actress, Cedric placed a decidedly possessive arm around Miss Cresswell's shoulders.

"I believe it is time I return Miss Cresswell home," he said in firm tones.

"Of course." Undaunted, Field once again kissed the fingers he held before stepping away. "Adieu, my beauty."

Not about to be outdone, Anna raised her hand to blow a small kiss in Cedric's direction.

"Do not forget, my lord, we shall be staying at the Drake tonight," she purred.

Cedric offered a half-bow before steering Miss Cresswell into the trees. He deliberately waited until they were out of sight of the actors before allowing his arm to drop.

He had not cared for the intimate manner in which that ridiculous Field had been eyeing Miss Cresswell. In truth, he had been hard pressed not to grab the man's cravat and shake him senseless. A wholly unexpected sensation for a gentleman who was rarely provoked.

He might have suspected his irrational reaction was one of jealousy if the notion was not so nonsensical.

"Why, Miss Cresswell, I do believe you were flirting," he drawled in a deliberately light tone.

She glanced up in obvious surprise at his accusation. "I was not."

"I distinctly saw you bat your lashes at that lecherous Romeo."

"I have never batted my lashes at anyone," she denied, then her gaze narrowed. "Besides, I at least did not make plans to meet him at the Drake."

His irritation vanished as swiftly as it had arisen.

So, the lovely minx had noted Anna's blatant invitation and was clearly displeased.

Good, he thought with a small smile.

It was only fair that she, too, was plagued with such odd sensations.

"I recall no plans to visit the Drake," he assured her.

"You are not going?"

"Why would I?" He deliberately lowered his gaze to the lips that all too frequently invaded his thoughts. "I have no interest in such obvious lures. I prefer a more subtle enchantment."

Her breath caught before she managed a chiding expression. "Now who is flirting?"

"So you have noticed?"

"Really, sir, you are impossible."

Suddenly overwhelmed by the need to have her close, Cedric deliberately steered them away from the lane.

"Here, we shall take a shorter path," he said, then, as they came to the edge of the trees, he swiftly turned to scoop her up in his arms.

She instinctively stiffened as he began to carry her across the parkland toward the garden.

"What are you doing?"

"This is Bart's favorite spot for treasure hunting," he explained, pressing her form as tightly as he dared to his chest. Those delectable lips were close enough to plunder with his own, but he manfully resisted temptation. The unpredictable Miss Cresswell was as likely to bloody his nose as to respond to the attraction between them. "I would not like you to injure your poor ankle after it has just healed."

She was not fooled for a moment. "I am perfectly capable of avoiding a large hole in the ground."

"We cannot take any chances. Besides, as you must know by now, I like having you in my arms."

"My lord," she protested.

"Yes, Miss Cresswell?"

Meeting his teasing gaze, she heaved a sigh. "Nothing."

Far too swiftly they had reached the garden, and with a slow reluctance he lowered Miss Cresswell to her feet. He felt somehow complete when he held her so close, as if she were the only woman who truly belonged in his arms.

"Here we are," he murmured. "Safe and sound."

She smoothed the folds of her skirts, her gaze not quite meeting his own.

"Are you coming in to speak with Lady Hartshore?"

"Not today, I think." He reached out to brush a stray curl from her cheek. There was more than a little temptation to linger in the company of Miss Cresswell, but Cedric was all too aware that he had begun to neglect the duties of his estate. Worse, he was not even certain that he cared. "I will call later, my dear."

Turning, Cedric forced himself to walk away.

It was that, or pulling her into his arms once more.

Eight

She would not look.

Seated at the window of the back parlor, Emma fiercely attempted to concentrate on the invitations to the Valentine ball that she was tying with pretty ribbons.

It was absurd.

There was certainly nothing to be seen out the foggy panes.

Indeed, there had been nothing to see the past three days. Surly gray clouds had blotted the sun and shrouded the countryside in an icy drizzle. Even the hardiest souls preferred the comfort of a warm fire to braving the raw wind.

And yet, on a hundred separate occasions Emma had discovered herself unwillingly drawn to the nearest window to search the lanes for signs of an approaching form.

No, not just a form, a renegade voice whispered in the back of her mind. The form of Lord Hartshore.

Emma tossed the invitation in the nearly overflowing basket.

She was being a fool.

What did she care if Lord Hartshore had apparently forgotten her very existence?

Hadn't she already determined that he was far too dangerous for her peace of mind? He was too dangerous for any sensible maiden.

It was decidedly for the best that he chose to remain far from Mayford. Ignoring what might have been a pang of regret, Emma reached for the last invitation.

At least she was nearly finished with the massive task of preparing the invitations, she reassured herself. It had been quite a chore with Lady Hartshore's demands that each one possess an original verse and be trimmed with lace.

And, of course, each invitation was a potent reminder that the Valentine ball had gone from a passing fancy to an inevitable fact.

She resisted the urge to sigh again as she tied the ribbon and dropped it into the basket.

No doubt it was the weather making her so blue-deviled, she told herself. It was certainly unlike her to brood in such a manner.

It was with a sense of relief that she heard the door to the parlor open, and rising to her feet, she watched Lady Hartshore cross the floral-patterned carpet to peer at the basket.

If anyone could distract her unwelcome thoughts, it was this woman.

Clapping her hands together, the countess regarded Emma with pleasure.

"Oh, my dear, the invitations are lovely."

"Thank you."

"I shall have them delivered today," Lady Hartshore decided in her abrupt style. "Now we must turn our attention to the decorations. What do you think of turning the ballroom into the forest of 'A Midsummer Night's Dream'? The ceiling could be draped in a spangle cloth with gauze on the walls and the columns decorated as trees. And, of course, the servants would be attired as various fairies. . . ." She paused as she pondered the magical event. "Do you suppose we could convince Bart to come as Puck? How charming for him to mingle among the guests quoting Shakespeare. 'Cupid is a knavish lad, thus to make poor females mad.' "

Emma was forced to bite her lip at the mere notion of the large, rather gruff gentleman playing the role of Puck. She could not imagine anything more absurd.

"I would be very much surprised," she said gently.

Lady Hartshore appeared to come to the same conclusion as herself, and she gave a tiny shrug.

"No matter. We shall find someone. And what of you, my dear? Have you decided upon a costume?"

Emma gave a small shudder at the mere thought. "Actually I believe that it would be inappropriate for me to attend at all."

"Absurd. Everyone will be most eager to meet you. Besides, I shall need you at my side."

"Really, I would prefer—"

"What of Delilah? Or perhaps Cleopatra?" The countess overrode her protest with bland indifference. "No, something more subtle. Perhaps Rosalind or Helen of Troy? Well, I shall no doubt think of something lovely."

"Please do not go to any effort on my behalf, Lady Hartshore. I would be much more comfortable in my own gown."

A rather worrisome smile played around the older woman's mouth. "We shall see. Now, what of refreshments?" She abruptly turned the conversation. "Champagne, of course, and for dinner we can safely depend upon Mrs. Borelli. Perhaps she will make the tarts in the shape of a cupid. Or something with hearts. It shall all be most romantic."

Emma barely prevented a grimace. "Yes."

"And perhaps you will find your own true love," the woman said in coy tones.

A surprisingly sharp stab of pain clenched Emma's heart. Ridiculous, considering she had already reconciled herself to the knowledge that she would never be in a position to fall in love. She was content with the path she had chosen, she fiercely reminded herself. Quite, quite content.

"I have no desire to find true love," she forced herself to declare.

Lady Hartshore gave a tinkling laugh. "My dear, I fear Cupid takes little interest in whether we wish to be struck by his arrow or not. I certainly did not intend to fall in love with Fredrick. I had already captured a very charming duke, when he strolled into my mother's drawing room and I was lost." She paused and tipped her head to one side. A clear indication that she believed her deceased husband was speaking to her. "Yes, yes, Fredrick. I have never regretted my choice. What is being a duchess compared to a life filled with happiness?"

Ignoring Lady Hartshore's conversation with her private ghost, Emma gave a shake of her head.

"Cupid rarely aims his arrows at companions, thank goodness."

"I sense you might be in for a surprise."

For no comprehensible reason, the thought of a dark countenance with a pair of golden eyes flared in Emma's mind.

With a sharp motion she turned to collect the large basket. "Shall I take these to Mallory?"

A speculative smile curved Lady Hartshore's mouth, but she gave a nod of her head.

"If you would be so kind."

"Of course."

With brisk motions Emma left the room and went in search of the butler. She was in no hurry to see the invitations delivered, but she had no desire to remain in the room discussing some imaginary gentleman whom Lady Hartshore had fancifully conjured.

For goodness' sake, gentlemen did not tumble into love with drab companions. Especially not drab companions who also happened to be the daughter of a notorious jewel thief.

It would not matter what costume she wore to the Valentine ball.

Stepping into the foyer, she discovered Mallory advising a young footman on his proper duties. At her arrival he dismissed the servant with a wave of his hand.

"Miss Cresswell."

"Lady Hartshore requested that these be delivered today."

The butler gave a ready nod of his head. "I shall see to it at once."

"Thank you." With a smile Emma turned to retrace her steps to the parlor. She had nearly reached the door, when a sharp bark echoed through the hall. With a frown of bewilderment Emma continued down the corridor and turned the corner to discover a familiar puppy wagging his tail in greeting. "Pudge, good heavens, how did you get in here?"

She reached down to grab him, only to stumble forward when he abruptly turned around and raced down the hall. She gave an impatient click of her tongue as she set off in pursuit. Certainly Lord Hartshore must be consumed with worry at his missing pet. She had to capture the dog before he became truly lost.

Of course, catching the puppy was easier said than done. Hampered by her heavy skirts, she could barely keep pace as Pudge scrambled through the west wing and turned to the short hall that led to the conservatory.

Emma breathed a sigh of relief at the knowledge that Pudge would be trapped. There was only one entrance to the pretty glass-and-wrought-iron structure. Once she had closed the door, his game would be at an end.

Stepping into the conservatory, Emma firmly closed the door behind her. Then, turning around, she searched for sight of Pudge.

It took only a moment to find him happily settled next to a pair of glossy Hessians. Emma's breath caught as her gaze traveled up the boots, the casual buckskins, and the form-fitted mulberry coat. At last she encountered the glittering golden gaze.

"My lord," she breathed in shock.

He slowly smiled down at her. "I had hoped this beast would lead you to me."

She blinked in astonishment as she realized this gentleman had deliberately used Pudge to lure her to the conservatory.

No doubt she should be furious at his deceit. It was hardly proper behavior for a respectable gentleman.

But what she felt was not fury. Instead, there was a wholly unreasonable tingle of pleasure rushing through her.

Suddenly all of the restless dissatisfaction that had plagued her for days vanished as the morning mist beneath the blaze of the sun.

"What are you doing here?" she asked.

"Ah, it is a surprise, of course."

Emma gave a shake of her head. Until meeting Lord Hartshore she had discovered most surprises to be singularly unpleasant. A predictable legacy of living with the Devilish Dandy.

"Yet another surprise?" she quipped.

He lifted his hands in an elegant motion. "What is life without surprises?"

"Peaceful?" she suggested.

His smile widened at her swift retort. "Dull," he corrected her, reaching out to take her hand and lead her toward the back of the conservatory.

Not about to be outdone, Emma tilted her head to meet his teasing gaze.

"Harmonious."

"Insipid."

"Content."

"Tedious."

The words hovering on her lips went unspoken as they passed a bank of flowers and she spotted the table set beside the glass panes. Covered with a pretty cloth, it was graced with a large wicker basket as well as two champagne glasses already filled.

"Oh."

He glanced down at her startled expression. "Although my cook cannot compare with Mrs. Borelli, she is thought to possess her own share of talent. Will you join me?"

Emma abruptly realized that she was quite alone with Lord Hartshore. And that she had thoroughly forgotten to treat him with the cool aloofness that she assured herself was only proper.

Still, it was the realization that she very much wanted to share this secluded picnic with Lord Hartshore that made her hesitate.

"Lady Hartshore will be expecting me."

"Mallory will inform her where you have disappeared to."

So, he had included the servants in his secret plot, she acknowledged, uneasily wondering what they thought of such an unconventional tryst. Of course, working at Mayford ensured the staff was prepared for the unconventional.

"You appear to have it all planned."

His expression became wry. "I have learned not to depend upon chance with you, Miss Cresswell. A well-plotted strategy seemed to be wise."

Emma briefly glanced toward the table before slowly returning her attention to the gentleman at her side.

"Why?"

He appeared caught off guard by her abrupt question. "What do you mean?"

"Why have you gone to such trouble?"

It took a moment before he at last gave a shrug. "Because it pleases me."

"That is no answer."

"Does it matter?"

"I believe it does," she admitted slowly.

He reached out to place a finger beneath her chin. "Do you fear I possess nefarious intentions?"

"No," she swiftly denied. Lord Hartshore might be dashing and unpredictable, but she never doubted that he was a gentleman. "Of course not."

"Good, because I do not steal the virtue of innocent maidens," he said softly. "Even if they are wood nymphs."

"It just seems that you would possess a better means of spending your afternoon," she persisted.

The golden eyes darkened before he gave a slight shake of his head, as if he had no desire to ponder whatever thought had suddenly struck him.

"There are few gentlemen who could think of a better means of spending an afternoon than with a beautiful lady." His tone was light as he dropped his hand and nodded toward the table. "Shall we?"

Emma was far from certain that she should remain. It was true she had no fear for her virtue. Or even her reputation. But the prickling sense of excitement she felt whenever she was in this gentleman's company seemed utterly improper.

And even a bit dangerous.

Yes, she really should return to the parlor and Lady Hartshore, she told herself, but even as she made her decision, her treacherous feet were carrying her toward the table. In the blink of an eye she was settled on the wrought-iron seat with no notion of how it occurred.

Swift to take advantage of her momentary bout of insanity, Lord Hartshore took his seat opposite her and began unloading the basket.

"Let me see what I can tempt you with," he teased, filling two plates with the large bounty. "Buttered lobster, potatoes in cream sauce, carrots, beef olives, cheese, and what appears to be a custard."

Emma accepted the proffered plate with the rueful knowledge she was destined to act out of character in this gentleman's company.

Common sense might tell her to flee, but the renegade desire to remain had won the day.

Picking up her fork, she glanced at the sinfully irresistible food set before her.

"Did you request your cook to feed the entire neighborhood?"

"No, just one slender maiden who looks as if a wayward breeze might topple her over." He once again reached into the basket to remove a perfect pink rose that he set beside her plate. "For you."

"Thank you," she whispered, feeling that dangerous prickle race through her body. Egads, it was no wonder she did not know if she was up or down. He managed to make her feel as if she were the most special creature in all of England. What maiden, no matter how sensible, could resist?

The sound of an off-key baritone voice belting out a rather naughty ditty was a welcome distraction, and Emma peered out the glass to discover Bart digging not far from the conservatory.

"Oh, there is Mr. Carson."

"I fear that singing is not his greatest talent," Lord Hartshore admitted with a wince. "Still, what he lacks in skill he more than compensates with his enthusiasm."

"Yes."

Lord Hartshore shrugged. "It makes him happy."

Reaching for her champagne, Emma turned her gaze back to the gentleman across from her.

"Have you ever attempted to halt him from his diggings?"

His brows rose. "Why should I?"

"Because there is nothing to find."

He leaned back in his seat with a nonchalant movement. "How do we know he might not stumble across some treasure or other? Besides, it is the search that pleases him. Do we all not search for some treasure in our life? Fortune, notoriety . . . love?"

Emma was forced to concede that she had not considered the matter in that particular light.

"Yes, I suppose so."

The golden gaze swept over her pale features. "What treasure do you hope to discover, Miss Cresswell?"

She did not have to ponder the question. "Security."

"A worthy goal."

"But dull," she challenged, knowing that few would ever comprehend her burning need.

Astonishingly, a somber expression descended upon his dark countenance.

"I suppose that rather depends upon whether one possesses it or not. Like most luxuries, we take it for granted until it is gone," he said in low tones. "I recall enough of my parents' habit of appearing and disappearing from my life to sympathize with the fear of not knowing what the morrow might bring. It was Aunt Cassie who at last brought me comfort."

Her heart skipped at his gentle understanding. "And what do you search for?"

He considered for a moment before replying. "Happiness, I suppose. Pleasure, beauty . . . love."

"Love?"

"Does that surprise you?"

It did, Emma acknowledged. Among fashionable Society, gentlemen rarely admitted the need for such an emotion. Indeed, it was often frowned upon as a symbol of weakness. Of course, this gentleman was hardly the traditional sort, she wryly reminded herself. His strength came from deep within and was not dependent upon what others thought of him.

She felt a pang of envy at his natural confidence.

"I would think if you were searching for love, you would travel to London."

"Why?"

"There are any number of suitable young maidens to chose from in town," she said, pointing out the obvious.

An odd expression descended upon his lean features. "You think one can shop for love as if it were a new coat?"

She was taken aback by his probing question. "Well, they do refer to the Season as the Marriage Mart."

"Ah, but choosing a proper bride and falling in love are two entirely different matters." He leaned forward, bringing him close enough that the heat and scent of him seemed to surround her. "I have no interest in the herd of debutantes being auctioned to the highest bidder. I wish to possess the same magic that Cassie and Fredrick shared."

For no reason, a sharp pang assailed her at the thought of some beautiful maiden bewitching this gentleman.

She set down her fork, her appetite suddenly absent.

"And you believe you will find such a maiden in Kent?"

"Actually I trust in Fate to drop her at my very feet."

There was something in his husky tone that had her gaze lowering to her half-empty plate.

"I wish you luck."

His chuckle sent a shiver down her spine.

"Thank you. I have a premonition that I shall need

it." There was a rustle, then a bowl of ripe strawberries was waved beneath her eyes. "Some fruit?"

She was saved from the necessity of answering as the door to the conservatory opened and a flustered Lady Hartshore made her way to the table.

At her arrival, both Emma and Lord Hartshore rose to their feet.

"Oh, Cedric, my dear," she cried in distress. "Forgive me for intruding on your lovely luncheon."

"We were just finishing," Lord Hartshore assured the older woman. "What has occurred?"

"I was sitting in the back parlor, enjoying a lovely cup of tea, when that dreadful . . ." Her words trailed away as her gaze landed upon the table. "Is that lobster?"

Tossing Emma an amused glance, Lord Hartshore obligingly reached for the platter of lobster.

"Yes, indeed it is. Would you care for a taste?"

Lady Hartshore eagerly reached out to take the buttered delicacy.

"Well, perhaps just a taste."

Lord Hartshore reached for another plate. "Some custard?"

She reached out her hand, only to pull it hastily back. "Oh, it looks so tempting, but Fredrick says that custards always give me nightmares."

Lord Hartshore's lips twitched again, but he readily set aside the dangerous custard.

"Well, we cannot have that."

Lady Hartshore heaved a sigh. "No, I suppose not."

"Was there a reason for seeking me out, Aunt Cassie?" he prompted gently.

"Of course. How silly of me," Lady Hartshore exclaimed, returning the lobster to the table. "That wretched vicar has called."

Emma grimaced, but Lord Hartshore merely shrugged. "I suppose it was inevitable."

"Yes," Lady Hartshore mourned, then visibly brightened. "Although his companion appears delightful enough. And quite handsome."

Sensing the flighty countess was distracted once again, Lord Hartshore steered her back to the purpose of seeking him out.

"Do you wish me to rid you of your unwelcome guest?"

Lady Hartshore pressed her hands together. "If you would, my dear. I must ensure that Mrs. Borelli does not do anything foolish."

"I shall be along in a moment," Lord Hartshore promised.

"Thank you, Cedric." With a grateful smile Lady Hartshore scurried away. No doubt pondering how to hide the most deadly knives from the ready hands of her volatile cook.

With a rueful grimace Lord Hartshore turned back to the silent Emma.

"It appears our interlude is at an end," he apologized. He held out his arm. "Shall we become St. George and rid Mayford of its dragon?"

"Perhaps I should help Lady Hartshore." Emma belatedly recalled her duty to her employer.

Reaching out, he firmly placed her hand upon his arm. "Oh, no, I refuse to do battle with the vicar without the support of flanking troops. Besides, your presence will ensure that I do not prove to be more dangerous than Mrs. Borelli."

Emma allowed herself to be led from the room, flashing him an amused smile.

"You could always take Pudge. He clearly is accustomed to your devious tactics."

He gave a bark of laughter. "I fear the last occasion Pudge encountered Mr. Allensway, he possessed the poor taste to . . . er . . . relieve himself upon the man's new shoes. I doubt if he has managed to conjure the Christian spirit of forgiving and forgetting."

She tried to choke back her laugh at the image of Pudge happily soaking the vicar's shoes.

"You are making that up," she accused the earl.

"I wish I were." Lord Hartshore heaved a mocking sigh as they made their way through the corridor. "Mr. Allensway condemned poor Pudge to the netherworld."

Emma gave a shake of her head. Although she should no doubt regret whatever weakness had prompted her to join Lord Hartshore in the conservatory, she could not conjure the elusive emotion. Instead, she knew that she would tuck the memory of their afternoon together along with their other shared moments in a secret portion of her mind. Memories that would be pulled out when she was far from Kent to bring brightness to a dark day.

Reaching the front parlor, he flashed her an encouraging smile before they stepped through the door. At their entrance, two gentlemen rose to their feet.

Emma gave the vicar a cursory glance before turning her attention to the tall gentleman with long, gray hair pulled back from his thin countenance in a velvet ribbon. A heavy mustache covered his upper lip and a pair of thick glasses distorted his green eyes. He was attired in somber black with an ebony cane in one hand.

As Lady Hartshore claimed, he was a handsome gentleman. A gentleman who might have graced any proper drawing room.

But at the sight of the stranger Emma felt her heart slam to a halt and her knees threaten to buckle.

This was no gentleman.

This was the Devilish Dandy.

"No . . . oh, no," she whispered.

Nine

For a dreadful moment Emma feared that her knees might give way and she would crumple to the floor.

Heavens above, why had her father followed her to Kent?

Hadn't she made it grimly clear when he had returned to London that she had no desire to see him?

She had ignored his every message. She had avoided visiting Sarah when she feared he might be in her home. She had even halted her regular trips to Hatcher's with the knowledge he might attempt to seek her out there.

Why the blazes could he not leave her in peace?

Unaware of the undercurrents in the air, the vicar stepped forward and cleared his throat in a self-important fashion.

"My lord, how fortunate you are here. I have brought my guest, Mr. Winchell, to introduce him to your lovely aunt."

Unimpressed, Lord Hartshore gave a faint shrug. "I fear there has been a trifling incident below stairs that has demanded Lady Hartshore's attention."

The vicar's face paled to a pasty hue at the thought of Mrs. Borelli collecting her knives from the kitchen, but determined to impress his guest, he managed a weak smile.

"Ah . . . indeed. Well, no matter. I would be pleased

to make you known to Mr. Winchell. Mr. Winchell, this is the esteemed Lord Hartshore."

Emma clenched her hands as her father stepped forward. She did not fear he was about to expose her. He would not have arrived in Kent under the guise of the mysterious Mr. Winchell if he wanted others to know his true identity. There was, however, always the possibility that Lord Hartshore might recognize him as the notorious Solomon Cresswell. From there it was only a short leap to realize she was related to the jewel thief.

The mere thought was enough to make her heart freeze in horror.

Thankfully there was nothing more than mild curiosity as Lord Hartshore gave a faint bow.

"Mr. Winchell."

"My lord."

"And this is Lady Hartshore's companion, Miss . . . er . . ." The vicar gave his cravat an uncomfortable tug as he struggled to recall Emma's name.

Emma paid him no heed as her father moved to take her lifeless hand in his own.

"Cresswell," he completed for the vicar.

Emma's shaky knees abruptly stiffened at the manner Solomon was regarding her with such tender concern.

She was not fooled for a moment.

He obviously wanted something from her.

The question was . . . what?

At her side she felt Lord Hartshore shift in surprise. "You are acquainted?"

The Devilish Dandy smiled with elegant ease. "I have the pleasure of being an old acquaintance of Emma's father."

Emma thinned her lips in displeasure. How easily the lies tripped from his tongue. She firmly withdrew her hand from his grasp.

"What are you doing here?"

Undeterred by her pointed lack of warmth, Solomon stroked the smooth ebony cane.

"The bishop requested that I visit the neighborhood, and, as you know, I have always preferred being in the country," he promptly explained, blithely ignoring the fact that he had never encountered a bishop in his scandalous life and that he had always adamantly professed a rousing distaste for the country. "What a pleasant surprise to discover such an old friend already in residence."

"A surprise, indeed," Lord Hartshore abruptly intruded, clearly beginning to sense there was something odd in the tension between her and Mr. Winchell. "I believe that you have just come from London?"

Solomon allowed the faintest glint to enter his eye at the gentleman's sharp question.

"In a rather roundabout route. I have recently visited the estate of Lord Chance, not far from here. He is currently in residence with his mother and fiancée."

Emma caught her breath. When she had left London, Sarah had not mentioned she would be traveling to the countryseat of her soon-to-be-husband, Lord Chance. Somehow the thought that her sister was so close provided a measure of comfort.

"They are well?" she asked before she could halt the question.

Her father gave a teasing grimace. "Quite well and so disgustingly happy, they are unbearable to be around. Even Lady Chance appears to be delighted with the upcoming nuptials."

Emma could not have been more pleased. There had been no doubt that Lord Chance was completely besotted with Sarah. And who could possibly blame him? She was beautiful, kind, and utterly giving of herself. But Lady Chance had been far less keen to allow the daughter of the Devilish Dandy into her family.

Emma knew that Sarah must be deeply relieved to have her approval before the wedding.

"I am pleased to hear so," she murmured.

"As am I," Solomon agreed before turning toward the gentleman regarding him in a suspicious fashion. "My lord, although I have been here a brief time, I have heard a great deal of you. The tenants are very proud to speak of the kind and generous earl."

Lord Hartshore's expression did not soften despite the obvious attempt at flattery.

"I consider them more friend than tenant," he said in firm tones.

Solomon gave an admiring nod of his head. "A worthy sentiment."

The vicar pressed himself forward, determined to share his own views on the subject.

"Yes, indeed, although it would not do to encourage those of lesser birth to imagine themselves as equals with their betters," he declared in stern tones. "They can be so encroaching, do you not think, Mr. Winchell?"

A decided frost fell upon the Devilish Dandy's thin features as he turned to regard his current host.

"I think we are all God's creatures, Mr. Allensway," he said with a slow emphasis. "And I do not recall that when God requested that we love our neighbors, he specified only those of noble birth."

Although obtuse to the true spirit of charity, Mr. Allensway possessed enough self-preservation to realize he had not pleased the gentleman he believed to hold his future in his hands.

"No, of course not. I merely meant that I would not wish to see discontent among the lower classes."

The Devilish Dandy was not about to let him off so easily. "Discontent comes from empty bellies and lack of hope, not from the hand of kindness. I trust your charitable efforts have taught you as much?"

The vicar paled, no doubt realizing that kind and charitable were two words that would never be applied to him.

"Yes, of course."

An awkward silence fell before Lord Hartshore was smoothly stepping into the breach.

"Will you be staying long, Mr. Winchell?"

"That rather depends." Solomon returned his gaze to Emma's pale face. "I have a certain duty to perform before returning to London."

So, she was right, Emma seethed. He did want something from her. Although she could not imagine what it could be. She had no money and nothing of value beyond . . . of course! Her emerald pendant.

"You make it sound quite mysterious," Lord Hartshore was saying as Emma glared at her father.

Solomon shrugged. "More delicate than mysterious, my lord."

Lord Hartshore gave a grunt, clearly dissatisfied by the evasive response.

"And it is your first visit to Kent?"

"I was here some years ago. Indeed, I once stayed for several weeks not far from here."

"Then perhaps you will encounter more than one old acquaintance among the neighbors."

Solomon smiled, although his expression was one of disbelief.

"Perhaps."

Emma shuddered at the mere thought. Good heavens, she could not bear another round of finger-pointing and cold shoulders. Of seeing the horror in Lord Hartshore's golden eyes.

Pressing a hand to her erratic heart, Emma realized that she had to be alone. She had to think of what she was to do. More important, she had to regain her com-

posure before she revealed just how distressed she was
by the arrival of Mr. Winchell.

"I must see to Lady Hartshore," she muttered, beginning to back toward the door.

Predictably, her father was not about to allow her to
escape so easily.

"Miss Cresswell, I hope you will consent to a brief
visit tomorrow? We have much to discuss."

Emma's hand instinctively clasped the emerald pendant. She did not want to hear what it was her father
wished to discuss. She just wanted him to disappear as
swiftly as he had appeared.

"My duties keep me very occupied."

His smile never wavered. "I am certain that Lady
Hartshore would not begrudge an old acquaintance a few
moments."

Vividly aware of Lord Hartshore's probing gaze and
the gathering frown upon the vicar's brow, Emma had
little choice but to agree.

"Very well. Now you must excuse me."

Refusing to allow another opportunity to be halted,
Emma whirled on her heel and fled the room.

Blast the Devilish Dandy.

Would she never be free of him?

Cedric watched Emma's abrupt departure with a growing sense of unease. Something was troubling her. Something connected with Mr. Winchell.

And he intended to discover precisely what it was.

"I will return in a moment," he promised with a hasty
bow, uncaring that it was hardly polite to leave the guests
on their own.

Swiftly following in her wake, Cedric caught sight of
her as she disappeared into the library. Within moments

he had joined her in the book-lined room and firmly shut the door behind her.

Hearing the click of the latch, Miss Cresswell abruptly turned to regard him with wide eyes. Within a heartbeat her expression was effectively guarded.

"My lord."

He moved to stand before her rigid form. "What is troubling you?"

"Nothing," she readily lied, her hands clenched at her sides.

"Mr. Winchell appeared to upset you."

"That is absurd."

Cedric drew in an annoyed breath. Why did she have to be so blasted independent? Could she not realize he simply wished to help?

"Miss Cresswell . . . Emma, I may not be a renowned scholar, but I am not precisely stupid," he said gently. "You nearly fainted when you caught sight of Mr. Winchell."

She abruptly turned from him, as if she feared what he might read in her eyes.

"I was merely surprised to discover him in Kent."

"But the vicar specifically told us that Mr. Winchell would be visiting."

"I . . . did not recognize the name. It has been some time since we were acquainted."

Moving forward, he reached out a hand to stroke the line of her tense shoulder. He longed to pull her into his arms and hold her close, but he was wise enough to realize that he might only frighten her away.

"Emma, if you are in trouble or danger, you must know that you could tell me. I would do everything in my power to protect you."

He felt the fine tremor that shook her body. "There is nothing you can do."

His heart gave a painful jolt at the hint of despair in

her voice. Damn Mr. Winchell. If he discovered the man was indeed the cause of Emma's distress, he would beat him with his own cane.

"You have not allowed me to try," he pointed out in firm tones.

"Please, I am fine, my lord. You must return to your guests."

"Emma . . ."

"Excuse me."

With a speed that he had not expected, she was moving across the carpet and through a side door that led into a rarely used corridor. Cedric knew that he would never catch her before she had raced up the stairs and locked herself in her chambers.

He heaved a rueful sigh.

The day had begun with such promise.

He had devoted a great deal of time and attention to his surprise picnic. So much attention that he occasionally paused to wonder at his preoccupation with the delectable Miss Cresswell. After all, it was one thing to enjoy stealing a kiss from a beautiful maiden or to even be curious about the mystery surrounding her presence in Kent. But to spend three days plotting the best means of bringing a smile to her lips . . . well, that rather smacked of a gentleman who desired more than a passing flirtation.

He had managed to dismiss his niggling concern with the rationalization that Miss Cresswell was in dire need of a bit of pleasure in her life. She had been so obviously delighted with the passing theater troupe and even the simple roses he bestowed upon her. Soon she would be leaving for her dreary life as a companion. Surely it was his duty to provide her with some amusement before she was gone forever?

Cedric glanced toward the door, knowing he should return to the guests. It was hardly done to simply abandon them in the parlor. But at the moment he was in no humor to play the entertaining host. In fact, he very much feared that if he returned to the parlor, he might attempt to force Mr. Winchell to confess the truth of his arrival in Kent. Even if he had to choke it out of him.

With a shake of his head, he quit the library and used the servants' staircase to take him into the garden. His groom would bring home his carriage. He felt in dire need of a bit of fresh air to clear his thoughts.

He gave a small shiver at the sharp breeze, but hunching his shoulders, he followed the paved path to the parkland. He had just angled toward the copse of trees, when a sudden call had him glancing up in surprise.

"Ho, Cedric."

His heart sank at the sight of Bart leaning upon his shovel. He knew he could not pass by without at least a brief visit.

"Good afternoon, Bart." Cedric moved to regard the fine hole that the gentleman had created. "I see you have been busy."

"Aye, I am getting close. I feel it in my bones."

Cedric's smile was decidedly wry. "Then you are fortunate."

Although eccentric, Bart could be surprisingly perceptive on occasion.

"What's this? A bit blue-deviled on this fine day?"

More than a bit, Cedric acknowledged to himself. And the worse part was that he didn't know why.

It was not his concern if Emma knew Mr. Winchell far more intimately than a distant acquaintance. Or if his arrival had only deepened the shadows that she kept shrouded around her.

Had she not made it clear that she did not desire his assistance? That she would, indeed, prefer him not to meddle in her affairs?

So why was his mood suddenly as dark as a brooding thundercloud?

"Perhaps a bit," he reluctantly admitted.

Bart gave a loud snort. "Woman trouble, I make no doubt."

Cedric raised his brows at the unexpected accusation. "Why would you presume any such thing?"

"Only two things give a gentleman the blue devils. Losing a battle or tangling with a female. You haven't been in a battle, have you?"

"Only a mild skirmish with the vicar," Cedric admitted in dry tones.

"Then it is a female."

Cedric grimaced. "Miss Cresswell."

A glint of comprehension dawned in the older gentleman's eye. "Ah, the lovely companion."

"She is lovely," Cedric agreed. "And perverse and most certainly hiding some secret."

Bart abruptly straightened. "A spy?"

"No, nothing so dramatic."

Reassured he was not harboring a dastardly sneak, Bart shrugged.

"If she's not a spy, then her secrets be her own."

It was precisely what Cedric had told himself only moments before, but Cedric found it impossible to dismiss the maiden from his thoughts.

"They are too heavy a burden for such a young lady. She is so brittle from the strain, I fear she might shatter."

Bart leaned forward, as if able to read something within Cedric's expression. Then he gave a slow nod of his head.

"I begin to understand. A wounded sparrow."

"What?"

"As a lad, you were forever dragging home some poor creature that had been injured or was ill. Cassie was never certain what she might encounter when she entered your chambers."

A reluctant smile curved Cedric's lips as he recalled his small menagerie. Not a day passed without him caring for a half dozen different rodents, reptiles, and birds. It said something of Cassie's sweet temperament that she had not forbidden him to bring them into Mayford.

"Ah, yes, I recall her rather dramatic reaction to the frog that escaped to the drawing room."

"You believed you could save anything."

"It at least seemed my duty to make the attempt."

"Clearly you still feel it your duty," Bart said in pointed tones.

Cedric shrugged. It was a tidy explanation. Perhaps Emma did manage to stir his natural instinct to protect her from harm. But that certainly did not explain his fierce desire to pull her into his arms. Or the highly improper dreams that made him awaken with an aching sense of need.

"I doubt that Miss Cresswell would appreciate being likened to a stray animal."

Bart gave a knowing nod of his head. "Nor will she be so eager to be saved."

"So I have discovered."

With a sudden frown Bart reached out to place a hand on Cedric's shoulder.

"Be careful, lad."

"Of Miss Cresswell?" he demanded in surprise.

"No greater danger to a sensible gent than a damsel in distress," he explained.

"I merely dislike seeing her so troubled."

"Aye, that is how it always begins," Bart scoffed. "You do a kind deed and next you are popping around to see that she is well and next you are mooning about the color of her eyes or the manner she moves across the room. A wretched business."

Cedric ruefully acknowledged that there were worse things to moon over than eyes the color of emeralds and the graceful sway of slender hips.

"I would not think it all wretched," he confessed.

Bart's hand dropped as he gave a disgusted shake of his head. "Bah. You are as noddy as your uncle. He couldn't leap into the parson's mousetrap swiftly enough. I tried to tell him how it would be, but he claimed that he could not live without Cassie. Beef-witted, I say."

"Uncle Fredrick never appeared to rue his decision," Cedric could not resist pointing out.

Bart gave a disgusted shake of his head. "Like I said, beef-witted."

Cedric's lips twitched. "Perhaps."

His tone was offhand, but Bart's gaze slowly narrowed in an accusing manner.

"I recognize that expression."

"What expression?"

"You will walk the plank and be happy for it."

For no reason Cedric could imagine, he felt a rash of alarm tingle through his body.

"Do not toss me overboard too quickly, Bart," he warned.

"I fear you have tossed yourself over," the older man mourned. "There is nothing left but to wish you happy."

Cedric gave a click of his tongue. Only Bart could liken love to walking the plank, he told himself. Or to confuse the desire to help another as an unspoken declaration.

It was ridiculous.

"I must be off," Cedric muttered. "Good luck with your digging."

"Aye, and luck be with you, my poor boy."

Ten

Slipping into the small copse of trees, Emma heaved a sigh of relief. She was certain that she had not been spotted when she had slipped quietly from the house. At least not by Lady Hartshore or the distinguished gentleman who had just arrived at Mayford.

She had spent the entire morning on edge, waiting for her father to make his appearance. It had been too much to hope that he would have sensed her open lack of welcome and simply returned to London.

Solomon Cresswell considered no one but himself, and if he decided he wished to speak with his daughter, then nothing would stop him. Least of all concern for Emma's desire in the matter.

Moving deeper into the trees, she kept securely out of sight of the main house. She would wait at least half an hour, she decided, before returning. Surely within that time even her father would have come to the conclusion she did not wish to speak with him.

She paced through the pathways, turning to retrace her steps, and then started over again. She tried not to think of her father seated with Lady Hartshore, no doubt charming her with his easy wit. Or the knowledge his experienced eye was no doubt assessing the priceless works of art that were openly displayed throughout the house.

The mere thought was enough to make her shudder in dread.

"Good morning, Emma."

Startled out of her dark thoughts, Emma whirled around to discover the Devilish Dandy regarding her with a faint smile.

As yesterday, he was once again attired in a severe black coat and breeches, with those absurd glasses perched upon his nose. A startling change from his usual preference for brilliant silks and lace. Only the lazy amusement in the green eyes was familiar.

"Father. What are you doing here?"

"I did warn you that I would be calling today." He cast a placid gaze at the trees. "Which is why I presume you are hiding."

The accusation of cowardice scraped at her pride, even if it was true.

"I am not hiding."

"No?"

"No. I merely do not believe we have anything to say to each other."

His smile never faltered. "Surely you wish to know why I have come to Kent?"

Emma lifted her hand to her emerald pendant. "I presume you are either fleeing from the authorities or are in need of money. Those are the only occasions you seem to recall you possess daughters."

"Egads." The Devilish Dandy gave a startled laugh. "I see that time has not dulled that brutal tongue, Emma."

She struggled to ignore her pang of guilt. Solomon Cresswell had never given her any reason to trust him.

"Why should I not speak the truth?"

"I assure you that on this occasion I did not see you out for protection or to plead for a bit of the ready," he assured her wryly. "Indeed, I have come with every intention of offering you my assistance."

Far from reassured, Emma regarded him warily. Her father helped no one unless there was some reward in it for himself.

"Then I fear you have made a wasted journey. I desire nothing from you."

"Will you not at least allow me to explain?"

"Why should I?"

Emma heard him heave a faint sigh. "You are right, of course. I have always been a selfish beast with little consideration beyond my own desires. It was not until I was lodged in Newgate, contemplating my imminent death, that I realized how my sins have harmed my daughters. Until that moment it had all been a game. Now I wish to make amends."

Emma shuddered as she recalled those horrible days when they awaited the Devilish Dandy to be carted to the noose. Regardless of what he had done, she could not bear the thought of him dying in such a ghastly fashion.

Still, she was no guidable fool. It would take more than a passing brush with death to alter her father's frivolous disregard for others.

"Very pretty, but somewhat late, would you not say?"

"I do hope not, Emma. I may not be the father you desire, but unfortunately I am the only one you possess."

"I have done quite well without a father," she informed him crisply. "I am very capable of taking care of myself."

He gave a slow nod of acknowledgment. "Yes, I have always admired that about you, my dear. Such fierce independence."

"I had little choice."

"No, you didn't. But matters have changed now."

Her wariness only deepened at his smooth words. "What do you mean?"

"As I said, my delightful stay within the walls of Newgate was an enlightening experience." His expression became uncommonly somber as he studied her pale features. "I came to realize that there was nothing more important in my life than my daughters. I made a promise to myself that if I got out of there alive, I would do everything in my power to ensure their happiness."

Unsettled by the seeming sincerity in his voice, Emma wrapped her arms around her waist. Her father was a master at making others believe what he wished them to believe.

"Really? And how do you propose to do that?"

He remained immune to her prickly disbelief. "I wish to give you what you have always desired."

"What?"

"True independence."

Emma flinched as if she had been slapped.

How dare he?

How dare he mock the simple dream that meant so much to her?

"That is not amusing," she gritted out.

"It was not intended to be amusing." He reached up to pluck the absurd glasses from his nose. The green eyes glittered with a sudden intensity. "I wish to give you a monthly allowance. It will be large enough to ensure you can rent a house and even hire a proper companion to lend you all the respectability you desire."

Emma stumbled backward. It was not at all what she had been expecting. Good heavens, she would have been less shocked had he requested she help filch the crown jewels. That at least would have been in character with the Devilish Dandy.

But this . . .

With an effort Emma drew herself up straight. She did not know how her father had deduced how best to tempt her. Before this moment she would have laid odds he did not even know the color of her eyes. But she did know that she was not about to sell her forgiveness for a few hundred pounds.

"No."

Her father remained unperturbed by her sharp refusal. "You needn't fear the money was stolen from some poor wretch, Emma," he drawled. "It is a perfectly proper legacy from a great-uncle."

Her lips thinned. She did not give a fig where the money came from. She would not be beholden to this man.

"I do not need anything from you."

"We have already agreed upon your competence, my dear. I do not offer the money because I fear you are too dull-witted to manage without me. I merely wish you to have it as a gift."

Visions of the Trojan horse rose to mind.

"Why?"

He gave a rueful shrug. "Because I have been a horrid father. Because I do not desire to see you hiring yourself out as a common servant. Because I wish you to have a home."

Oh, he was good, Emma had to acknowledge wryly. There were no arrogant commands. No embarrassing pleas. No ultimatums. Just sweet temptation dangled before her like a fine wine before a drunkard.

It was little wonder he had enjoyed such a brilliant career.

"I do not need your charity."

"Charity? Really, Emma, I hardly consider a father supporting his daughter as charity."

"Perhaps not among most fathers and daughters. But ours is hardly a common relationship."

The Devilish Dandy readily smiled at her accusation. "No, I have never been of the common variety, but that does not make me any less your father."

She heaved an exasperated sigh at his tenacity. "I do not wish to argue with you. I have made my decision."

Her father reached out to brush her cheek in a familiar motion. "I have no desire to argue either, Emma, but neither do I intend to concede defeat. Sarah warned me that I should find it easier to teach cows to fly as to convince you to accept my offer. Thankfully, I am quite as stubborn as you. I shall remain in Kent as long as necessary."

She instinctively stepped form his touch, a frown marring her brow.

"You cannot continue to stay with Mr. Allensway."

Solomon grimaced. "A most daunting prospect, I must admit. He is a ghastly bore. Still, my willingness to endure such company should at least assure you of the sincerity of my desire to make amends."

Emma remained unimpressed. "You do realize that Mr. Allensway is expecting you to offer him a position?" she pointed out. "It is hardly kind to raise his expectations, only to dash them."

"Any expectations he is harboring are nothing more than a figment of his pompous imaginings," the Devilish Dandy retorted without remorse. "The bishop made no mention of a position in his letter. He merely requested that I be his guest for a short visit."

Emma gave a click of her tongue. "There is no bishop. I know quite well that you wrote that letter."

Solomon slowly raised his brows. "I fear I must disappoint you, Emma. It was indeed a genuine bishop who wrote the letter. He is an old friend of mine."

"You expect me to believe a bishop would be friends with a notorious jewel thief?"

"Oh, the irony is not lost on me," her father admitted with a wry smile. "However, in his defense, Francis was not a bishop when we first met. Indeed, we were both grubby school-lads who were far smaller than the other boys and inclined to be routinely bullied. We formed an alliance more out of survival than anything else. Over the years we remained close despite the bishop's disapproval of my chosen profession."

Irony, indeed, Emma acknowledged with an inward sigh. Trust the Devilish Dandy to be hand in hand with a bishop.

"And this bishop agreed to deceive a fellow man of the cloth so you could follow me to Kent?" she demanded in disapproving tones. "Hardly what one would expect from a leader of the Church."

Her prim words did nothing more than widen his smile.

"Francis is not so easily influenced by my wicked charm as that," he denied. "When he wrote the letter, the genuine Mr. Winchell had every intention of traveling to Kent. Of course, it was not for the purpose the vicar presumes. He was coming to determine whether the nasty rumors surrounding Mr. Allensway's indifference to his flock were true. The bishop is a stern believer that the Church is duty-bound to succor those in need. Unfortunately Mr. Winchell fell ill before he could undertake the task, and knowing I had already made plans to travel to Mayford, he requested that I take the place of Mr. Winchell. It was my own notion not to reveal I was not the guest the vicar was expecting. I feared that you might bolt if you learned I was coming."

As well she might have, Emma inwardly acknowledged. Had she been given the opportunity to brood upon the arrival of the Devilish Dandy, she was not certain even her promise to Lord Hartshore would have prevented her from fleeing Kent.

"Well, at least your visit will not be entirely wasted," she forced herself to say. "The bishop should be told of Mr. Allensway's wretched behavior."

"Oh, he will be told. But not until I have assured myself that you are happy."

Realizing that her father was preparing to renew his insistence that she accept his charity, Emma gathered her scattered wits.

She should have walked away the moment he had approached.

It would have been far less disturbing to continue with her belief he had pursued her for the emerald necklace.

"I must return to Mayford. Lady Hartshore will be expecting me."

"Emma." Her father reached out to grasp her arm. "At least think upon my offer."

"I must go."

Shaking off his hand, Emma moved swiftly through the trees.

Think upon his offer? Not bloody likely.

Heavens above. She had assumed she had troubles before. Ghosts, pirates, fortune-tellers, and irresistible lords seemed enough for any innocent maiden to bear. But suddenly they were all but inconsequential.

How could they possibly compare to a father disguised as an emissary for the bishop, who also happened to be a wanted jewel thief?

Her thoughts ran in circles as she let herself into the quiet house. What she needed was a cup of hot tea and a few hours in her chambers to soothe her tangled nerves, she decided. Or better yet, a healthy sampling of the fine brandy Lady Hartshore kept beside her bed.

She certainly would not be the first person the Devilish Dandy had driven to the bottle.

Her feet were already leading her up the wide flight of steps, but even as she turned to continue up to her chambers, she discovered herself hesitating upon the landing.

It was odd, but the offhand thought of her employer had sent an icy chill down her spine.

An unconscious frown tugged at her brows as Emma attempted to dismiss the ludicrous sensation.

She had seen Lady Hartshore only an hour before, and she had been in high spirits. In fact, she had been happily chatting about her plans for the upcoming ball and her intention to spend the afternoon sketching her ideas for decorating the ballroom.

Still, she could not force herself to continue her path to the upper rooms.

Blast, she was being absurd, she told herself as she moved down the corridor toward the maid busily dusting a pier table. Her unease was no doubt a symptom of her confrontation with her father.

Unfortunately she knew she would not be able to go to her rooms until she had assured herself that Lady Hartshore was comfortably settled with her sketches.

"Sally, do you know where I can find Lady Hartshore?" she asked of the servant.

Pausing in her dusting, the maid gave a jerk of her head toward a distant door. "In the library, miss."

"Thank you."

Emma continued her way down the corridor, that icy prickle growing more pronounced the closer she came. By the time she reached the library, she was nearly running.

Muttering at her foolishness, she pushed open the door. She thoroughly expected to discover the countess seated at her delicate desk or even stealing a nap upon the chaise longue.

What she found instead was Lady Hartshore lying next to the fireplace with a trickle of blood running from a wound on her forehead.

For a moment Emma was frozen with shock.

Surely the good lady had not been attacked in her own

home? It was unthinkable. And yet, what other explanation was there for the ugly cut and her state of unconsciousness? Unless she had fainted and hit her head . . .

Her rambling confusion was abruptly thrust aside as her wide gaze traveled over the limp form and came to rest upon the full skirts of Lady Hartshore's bombazine gown. Unexplainably, the grate had been removed from the front of the smoldering fire and the full skirts had fallen close enough to the coals to have been set ablaze.

With a cry of alarm Emma dashed to her employer and, falling to her knees, she began beating out the flames with her hands.

"Sally," she cried out, praying the maid was still working in the corridor. She had no way of knowing how badly Lady Hartshore was injured. The cut did not appear life-threatening, but any blow to the head was dangerous.

Thankfully the startled maid appeared in the doorway in bare moments, her gasp echoing through the silent room.

"Cor . . . is she dead?"

"No," Emma snapped, ignoring the pain of her singed hands. "But she is in need of a doctor. Have Mallory fetch one immediately."

The maid dashed away, and Emma returned her attention to the wound upon Lady Hartshore's forehead. Withdrawing a handkerchief, she carefully dabbed at the sticky blood.

Debating whether or not to fetch the brandy to clean the cut, Emma felt a flare of profound relief as Lady Hartshore's lashes fluttered, then slowly lifted.

"Emma?" she whispered in confusion.

"Do not move. You have had an accident."

"An accident?"

"I believe so—"

"What has occurred?" a dark, decidedly concerned male voice intruded into Emma's words, and she glanced up to discover Lord Hartshore crossing the room with vast strides.

Emma had never been so happy to seen anyone in her entire life. In fact, she might have jumped up and kissed him if her shaky limbs would have supported her. Instead, she waited for him to drop down beside her before flashing him a relieved glance.

If anyone could be trusted in an emergency, it was this gentleman.

"Oh, my lord, I found your aunt unconscious on the floor. She is injured."

"Aunt Cassie, can you hear me?" Lord Hartshore demanded, his countenance unnaturally pale.

"Yes." Lady Hartshore raised a limp hand to touch the bump on her forehead.

"Do you know what happened?"

Surprisingly, a weak smile tugged at the older woman's lips. "I am not certain I wish to confess," she said in rueful tones. "It is so silly."

Emma exchanged a startled glance with Lord Hartshore before he lifted his aunt's hand to give it a warm squeeze.

"We would never think you silly, my dearest."

"But it was silly," Lady Hartshore protested. "I decided that the room had grown a bit chilled, and rather than bother the servants, I decided to stir the fire myself. Only when I bent down to retrieve the poker, I hit my head on the mantel."

"An accident that could happen to anyone," Lord Hartshore said softly. "But we must have someone see to that cut."

"I have sent Mallory for the doctor," Emma assured him swiftly.

He flashed her an appreciative glance. "Quite right. I shall carry her to her chambers." Reaching out to scoop his arms beneath his aunt, he suddenly stilled, his gaze trained on the blisters dotting the palms of Emma's hands. "What have you done?"

With a hint of embarrassment Emma abruptly buried her hands in the folds of her skirt.

"The hem of Lady Hartshore's dress had fallen into the fire."

Lord Hartshore's gaze flickered down to the badly charred material before returning to her face in disbelief.

"And you put the flames out with your hands?"

Emma shrugged. "I fear I was not thinking clearly."

Lady Hartshore gave a loud gasp. "But, my dear . . . you saved my life."

Lord Hartshore's gaze never wavered from Emma's growingly pink countenance.

"She did, indeed."

Emma shifted uncomfortably. "Nonsense."

"That is the reason Fredrick sent you to me," Lady Hartshore babbled, only increasing Emma's embarrassment. "He knew you would save me. How ever can I thank you?"

The sharp memory of the unease that had sent her in search of Lady Hartshore flickered through her mind. Could it be true? Had Lady Hartshore's dead husband managed to reach out from the grave to steer her to the library at precisely the moment Lady Hartshore was in peril? Had he brought her to Kent for just this moment?

Then common sense abruptly returned and she inwardly chastised her nonsensical thoughts.

It had been nothing more than coincidence.

A very lucky coincidence to be sure. But nothing unworldly about it.

"I did only what anyone else would have done," she said briskly, eager to divert the attention from herself. "You must allow Lord Hartshore to carry you to your room."

As if sensing her growing agitation, Lord Hartshore

scooped his aunt into his arms and raised himself to his feet.

"She is right, Aunt Cassie. You have a very nasty bump on your head."

The older woman turned to glance toward Emma, who struggled to her own feet.

"You will come with us, my dear?"

Although she felt shaky and in even greater need of that brandy she had promised herself earlier, Emma gave a nod of her head.

"Of course."

Following Lord Hartshore upstairs, Emma helped him settle Lady Hartshore onto her wide bed, then, assuring the older woman she would be close at hand, she stepped aside as half a dozen servants tumbled into the room.

Leaving the horde to moan and cluck over the wounded countess, Emma sought a chair in the far corner. Her knees still felt weak and now her toes ached from being trampled by Lady Hartshore's amply proportioned chambermaid.

With a sigh she leaned her head against the thick cushion. All in all, it had been quite an eventful day. Too eventful. First her father's shocking offer. And then finding Lady Hartshore lying on the library floor.

It was little wonder she felt drained, she acknowledged as she allowed her lashes to flutter downward. She continued to keep her eyes shut as the crowd in the bedroom swelled to include the gardeners, the groom, and at last the doctor. She ignored the loud chatter as she willed her heart to slow its frantic pace and her taut muscles to relax.

Emma had no notion how much time passed before her peace was disturbed by strong hands grasping her wrists to turn her palms upward. She abruptly opened her eyes to discover a tall, gaunt-faced gentleman regarding the angry blisters upon her skin with a practiced gaze. The same doctor who had so recently tended to her twisted ankle.

"Lady Hartshore tells me that you burned your hands, Miss Cresswell."

"It is nothing, I assure you."

Disregarding her protest, the doctor made a thorough examination of her hands before bending down to pluck out a clean cloth and bottle of foul-smelling liquid from his bag on the floor.

"Mmm . . . they will heal, but they must be kept clean and bandaged," he informed her as he efficiently set about wiping her tender palms. Then, reaching back into his bag, he withdrew a jar and began smearing a white ointment onto the burns. "This should help with the pain," he murmured as he set the jar aside and then wrapped thin strips of linen around her hands. "But the bandages must be changed every evening."

The pain had already begun to subside, but Emma gave a nod of her head. She knew from experience that there was little use arguing with this man.

"Very well."

Straightening, the doctor regarded her for a silent moment.

"You performed a most courageous deed today, Miss Cresswell. The entire neighborhood is in your debt."

Emma gave an awkward shake of her head, knowing that her actions had been performed more out of panic than courage.

"I am only relieved that I was in time."

"It was a miracle."

A faint smile softened Emma's tense features. "Or the work of Fredrick, if we are to believe Lady Hartshore."

Expecting the sensible doctor to chuckle at her words, she was surprised as he gave a rueful shrug.

"Perhaps it was. When you reach my age, Miss

Cresswell, you learn that there are many things in this world that we do not comprehend."

Before today Emma would have dismissed the mere notion with a loud snort. Now, remembering those forbidding chills, she could not so readily laugh aside the absurd sentiment.

"I suppose," she agreed in faint tones.

The doctor reached out to kindly pat her shoulder.

"You just concentrate on caring for those burns."

"Do not fear, doctor." Lord Hartshore abruptly appeared beside Emma's chair, his gaze trapping her own in a golden warmth. "I will ensure that she receives the greatest care."

Eleven

Cedric did not allow his gaze to waver from Emma's too-pale face. Not even when the good doctor performed a small bow.

"Then I shall leave my patient in your care," he murmured.

"Thank you."

Barely noting the discreet withdrawal of the older gentleman, Cedric reached down to gently brush a stray curl behind her ear.

A soft, poignant tenderness washed through him. He wished they were alone so that he could pull her into his arms and assure himself that she was truly unharmed.

When he had first entered the library, his thoughts had naturally been upon his aunt. He had been terrified that she had been overcome by some dread illness. But once assured that Cassie had suffered only minor injuries, his concern turned to Emma.

He felt her pain as if it had been his own hands burned. She had been a fool to battle the flames with such disregard for her own safety.

Certainly he was deeply grateful for her saving his aunt, but he could not deny a desire to shake her for putting herself in harm's way.

If she had been seriously hurt . . . gads, it did not even bear thinking of.

Growing uncomfortable beneath his steady regard, Emma shifted in the chair.

"How is Lady Hartshore?"

"Already complaining that she is far too busy to remain in bed. I believe she feels the world will come to a halt if she is not personally involved in keeping it spinning along."

Thankfully his light tone managed to coax a faint smile to her lips.

"I suppose that is a good sign."

"Yes, although she will no doubt attempt to bully the servants into allowing her to rise," Cedric retorted, all too familiar with his aunt's perverse nature. "I fear I will have to remain at Mayford to keep her from any sort of foolishness."

He was not at all surprised when she stiffened at his determined words.

"You intend to stay at Mayford?"

"You need not sound so horrified," he mocked softly.

That charming color instantly flooded her cheeks. "I was merely surprised."

"Who else will change your bandages?" he inquired, then, as her lips parted to protest, he pressed a finger to them. "Besides, I intend to ensure you do not risk yourself again performing heroic deeds."

"I did nothing heroic."

He leaned forward, his finger moving to trace the line of her stubborn jaw.

"You saved Cassie's life."

She trembled beneath his touch, but astonishingly she did not jerk away. Cedric could only presume that she was still in shock.

"I did nothing that you or even one of the servants wouldn't have done had you entered the library."

He gave a slow shake of his head. "Be modest if you

wish, but the truth is that my family owes you a debt that can never be repaid."

Her head ducked at his insistent words. "Please, I wish you would not talk such nonsense. It quite puts me out of patience."

"Well, we cannot have that." Cedric struggled to hide his amusement at her embarrassment. "I shall respect your wishes. However, I do insist that you devote the next few days to recovering from your injuries."

Her head rose abruptly at the firm command. "Lady Hartshore will need me to oversee her duties and, of course, I must keep her company. She will grow bored without some form of entertainment."

"I will keep my aunt entertained, and any duties can be safely laid upon the housekeeper," Cedric insisted.

She heaved a faint sigh of exasperation. "I assure you that I am perfectly fine."

"Nevertheless you are commanded to be at your leisure."

"I would really prefer—"

"That is an order, Miss Cresswell," Cedric informed her in stern tones.

The emerald eyes flashed with the temper she took such great care to hide.

"Yes, my lord. As you say, my lord."

He gave a sudden chuckle. "Very nice, my little wood nymph, but I unfortunately do not trust you to behave yourself any more than I trust my aunt to remain abed. I fear the moment I turn my back you will be down in the kitchen or fetching and carrying for Aunt Cassie."

"What do you propose to do? Tie me to my bed?"

Cedric caught his breath at the seductive, wholly improper image that rose to mind. He could no longer deny that he would dearly love to have her upon a bed. Any bed. The nearest bed. Although he did not wish to have her in any way bound. He wanted her free to wrap her arms around his back and her legs around his. . . .

Good gads. He took an abrupt step backward. He would have to gain greater control over his treacherous thoughts if he were to remain beneath the same roof with this woman for the next few days. Or at least remain very close to plenty of cold water.

"Well, if that is your desire, I should naturally do whatever necessary to accommodate you," he quipped in light tones. "However, I was thinking of nothing more outrageous than a simple promise to do as I request."

An unwanted awareness flickered through her eyes before she was giving an uncomfortable shrug.

"If you insist."

"I do," he said softly. "You have become far too important to my family to allow you to take unnecessary risks. Until those hands are completely healed, you are strictly off duty. Now I must return to Hartshore Park and pack a few belongings." He smiled into her wary eyes. "Do not fear, I shall return before you have the opportunity to miss me."

"Of that I have no doubt," she muttered.

Offering her a faint bow, he made his way out of Mayford. Before leaving the room, Cedric paused by the bed to assure his aunt he would soon return.

His carriage was waiting, and within moments he was swiftly on his way to Hartshore Park.

He leaned back into the squabs with a faint sigh.

Although it had been nothing more than a whim that had led him to Mayford, he was deeply relieved that he had not ignored it in favor of meeting with his growingly impatient steward. In truth, he cursed himself for taking so deuced long to choose between his dark gold coat and a more dashing one in green.

If not for his uncharacteristic bout of vanity, it would

have been him to discover Cassie in the library and Emma would not have been injured at all.

A wry smile abruptly twisted his lips.

If not for Emma, he would not have been plagued with indecision as to which coat best set off his shoulders, he acknowledged.

Gads, he was beginning to behave as ridiculous as any callow schoolboy. Twittering over his clothing, ignoring the demands of his estate, toting around roses in the off chance that he might encounter the vexing maiden, and spending his nights plagued with dreams that left him aching with need.

If he were not careful, he would end up walking the plank, just as Bart had predicted.

His absurd thoughts were at last interrupted as they drew to a halt before his home. Climbing from the carriage, Cedric intended to linger no longer than it took to reveal his intentions to his staff and toss a few belongings in his bag.

Unfortunately he had not counted upon his shocked valet, who insisted it would take every bit of an hour to properly pack all the belongings necessary for a gentleman of fashion to be gone overnight. Or his steward, who firmly demanded Cedric's approval before beginning the repairs on the gatehouse. Or even the distraught cook, who insisted that Lady Hartshore would go into decline without her special gruel.

All in all, it was nearly three hours before he was at last able to return to Mayford.

Leaving his bags to be unpacked in the guest chamber, he strolled into the back parlor to discover Mrs. Borelli awaiting him with a large tray set on a satinwood table.

"There you are," the servant said in brisk tones. "I have made you tea."

Although the large platters of sandwiches, sliced ham,

and pastries were tempting, Cedric gave a shake of his head.

"Thank you, Mrs. Borelli, but I am not very hungry at the moment."

The woman placed her hands on her hips. "A gentleman needs to keep his strength about him. I haven't time to nurse you as well. Now, eat."

Cedric was far too accustomed to Mrs. Borelli to be offended by her gruff command.

"I prefer to wait for Miss Cresswell."

"She will be down in a moment," the servant promised.

Cedric chuckled. "Meaning that you bullied her as well."

"Aye. And your aunt."

"How is she?"

The militant expression abruptly softened. For all her grumbling manner, Mrs. Borelli was utterly devoted to the countess.

"She will be on her feet in a day or two, thank God."

Cedric gave a nod of his head. "And thank Emma for going into the library when she did."

"Yes, Fredrick was right to bring her here," Mrs. Borelli agreed in sage tones.

Cedric was far from convinced that his deceased uncle had been responsible for Emma's presence at Mayford, but if it comforted the woman as well as his aunt, then he was content to allow them their beliefs.

"I must recall to thank him in my prayers."

"You should, indeed." A decidedly sly expression descended upon the round countenance. "And not just because of Lady Hartshore."

"What do you mean?"

"You will discover in good time," the cook promised, then, as if sensing the approach of another, she abruptly turned in time to watch Miss Cresswell uncertainly step into the room. "Ah, good. Tea is ready."

Neither Cedric nor Emma noticed the woman regarding them with a knowing gaze, or even her silent withdrawal from the room.

Slowly stepping forward, Cedric carefully studied the pale features that had become more familiar than even his own.

He could describe every curve, every line, every freckle scattered over her tiny nose. He could glance into the emerald eyes and know if she was happy or sad or angry. He could close his eyes and know she was near by the scent of her skin.

Now he sensed a tension within her that made him fear she might bolt rather than be alone with him.

Swiftly moving forward, he gently grasped her wrists and pulled her forward.

"Emma, I am glad you are here. How are you feeling?"

"I am fine," she assured him.

He lifted her hands to study the bandages. "Are they very painful?"

"No, indeed, they are already much improved—" Her words broke off as he impulsively bent his head to kiss the wounded palms. "My lord."

Lifting his head, he met her startled gaze. "Cedric," he insisted softly. "My name is Cedric. Say it."

A delightful confusion flickered over her face at his command, but rather than obey his order, she gave a faint shake of her head.

"I wish you would not make a fuss."

A wave of tenderness swept through him. He found it dangerously easy to fuss over this woman.

"I think it is time that someone did."

"I assure you it is not necessary."

"Perhaps I should be the judge of that."

She gave an uneasy tug of her hands, but he maintained his grip. He had no doubt she would scurry to the other end of the room given the opportunity. For the moment he needed her close, if only to reassure himself that she was well and safe.

"Have you seen your aunt?" she attempted to distract him.

"I stepped in earlier, but she was sleeping and I did not wish to disturb her. Mrs. Borelli has assured me that she is currently enjoying her tea. I shall check on her later."

There was no mistaking the genuine relief that lightened the emerald eyes. Whatever her determination to leave Mayford, it was evident she had become quite fond of Lady Hartshore.

"Good."

He smiled into her eyes. "And since she is so comfortably settled, I believe that we can safely enjoy our own tea. Shall we?"

She paused before giving a slow nod of her head. "Very well."

"Allow me."

With great care Cedric led her to a comfortable settee, then, assured she was close enough to the warmth of the fire, he filled a plate with sandwiches and a cup with the impressively hot tea. Choosing a glass of scotch that Mrs. Borelli had thoughtfully provided, Cedric relaxed into a chair close to the settee.

Sipping the fiery liquid, Cedric watched as Emma nibbled at a sandwich. Even in the fading light it was easy to detect the shadows beneath her fine eyes and the faint droop of her shoulders.

"You look exhausted," he said abruptly.

"I am tired," she admitted with a grimace. "Ridiculous, since I have done nothing but rest in my room the entire afternoon."

"Shock," Cedric informed her sagely. "It tends to affect one like that. One moment you seem to have an overabundance of energy, and the next you want nothing more than to lie down and sleep."

"Yes."

"You must take things slowly over the next few days."

She flashed him a dry smile. "I believe you have already ordered me to do so."

"True enough." He stretched out his legs and crossed them at the ankles. "It will not harm you to enjoy a day or two of ease."

"I have done nothing but be at my ease since arriving in Kent," she retorted in tart tones.

"And you look remarkably better for it. Your skin has acquired an exquisite glow and you no longer look as if you might disappear like a wisp of smoke." Cedric deliberately allowed his gaze to lower to her full lips. "Now, if we could just convince you to smile upon occasion."

She abruptly set aside her cup and plate. "You are being absurd."

Cedric chuckled at her maidenly confusion. What a delight she was to tease.

"More tea?"

She awkwardly rose to her feet. "No, I think I shall return to my room."

Pushing himself out of his chair, Cedric attempted to conjure some means of keeping her near. It seemed that she was always running from him. Just like the wood nymph Daphne remained just out of reach of the besotted Apollo. He felt a pang of sympathy for the ancient god. It was extraordinarily frustrating to desire something so elusive.

"I will be here if you are in need of me," he at last murmured, realizing that he could not force her to remain.

With a faint nod of her head Emma swept from the room, once again leaving Cedric to his own devices.

He very much feared he was simply deceiving himself to believe his only desire in Emma Cresswell was discovering the mystery of her presence in Kent.

Apollo, indeed, he thought wryly. Chasing after a wood nymph who had no intention of being caught.

Unwilling to brood upon his futile thoughts, Cedric set aside his glass and made his way to his aunt's room. He was relieved to discover her propped upon her bed with no seeming after-effects beyond a large lump upon her forehead. He pulled a chair close and allowed her to happily prattle for the next few hours. It was not until Mrs. Borelli entered the room and insisted that Lady Hartshore rest that he returned downstairs to share a casual dinner with Bart, followed by a leisurely game of chess.

By ten o'clock the household had fallen silent and Cedric concluded that there was little to be done beyond seeking his own bed. He had long since concluded that Emma was determined to keep herself hidden in her room. He did not relish sitting alone in the parlor, watching the fire fade to embers.

Pouring himself a glass of brandy, he climbed the stairs and was just passing Emma's room, when he heard a muffled cry echo through the heavy door.

With swift movements he shamelessly pressed his ear to the heavy door. For a moment there was nothing to be heard, and Cedric was on the point of continuing down the corridor, when another muffled cry decided his actions.

Without consideration to the impropriety of entering a maiden's bedchamber, he thrust open the door and hurried inside. The smoldering fire gave ample light to assure him that Emma was not under attack from some unknown intruder, nor had she fallen, as he had first feared.

Instead, she lay upon her bed, clearly in the throes of a nightmare that had her twisting her head upon the pillow and reaching out her hands as if to grasp at some elusive object.

Cedric knew he should leave. The maiden was clearly in no danger, except for having her reputation thoroughly shredded by his presence. But even as he told himself to quietly back out of the room and continue his journey to his own chambers, his unruly feet were carrying him forward.

With concise movements he placed himself on the mattress next to her and slowly drew her trembling body into his arms.

"Please, no," she moaned, clutching at his coat.

Pulling her even closer, Cedric ran a soothing hand over the fall of her golden hair. The feel of her slender frame curled next to his own with the warm scent of her filling his senses felt profoundly right. He knew at that moment he could hold her like this forever.

"Emma, I am here," he said softly.

"Father . . ."

"Shush, Emma, it is only a dream."

She shuddered, then the thick black lashes slowly lifted to reveal a pair of dazed emerald eyes.

"What?"

"You were having a bad dream," he explained gently.

Half expecting her to pull away in shock, he was pleasurably surprised when she merely gave a slow nod of her head.

"Yes, I was lost in a labyrinth and there was a man . . . I wanted him to help me find my way clear, but he kept disappearing."

Cedric recalled her desperate cry for her father. Emma had made a concerted effort to avoid discussing her family. He could only wonder what she was hiding.

"What man?" he asked in low tones.

"I don't know." Her brows furrowed as she struggled to recall the fading nightmare. "I thought for a moment it was my—" Her words stumbled to a halt before she attempted to cover her near slip. "I never saw but a glimpse of him."

Cedric did not doubt for a moment she knew the man to be her father. So why would she lie? It was nothing more than a dream. He carefully stored the question in the back of his mind to be pondered later. For now his only concern was easing the tension that still gripped her body.

With a gentle insistence he pressed the glass of brandy into her hands.

"Here, I think you are in more need of this than I."

Cautiously she lifted the glass to her lips to take a small sip.

"Ugh."

Cedric chuckled at her expressive revulsion. Hardly a compliment to Bart's fine cellar.

"It will help you relax," he assured her.

She took another reluctant sip. "It is worse than the tonics Sarah made me drink when I was a child."

"Sarah?"

Her features abruptly softened. "My sister."

"She cared for you when you were young?"

She gave a nod, the silk of her hair brushing his cheek in a most pleasant fashion. Before this moment Cedric would have sworn there was only one pleasurable means of spending time with a lady in her bed. Now he realized there was something infinitely satisfying in merely holding someone close.

"Yes, my mother died when I was just a child."

"I commend your sister. She did remarkably well raising you."

"It must have been very difficult for her to take on the role of mother when she was still but a child," Emma said in sleepy tones. "But I can never recall her complaining. I am not certain that I ever properly appreciated what she sacrificed for Rachel and me."

He retrieved the glass that threatened to slip from her fingers and set it aside.

"I am certain what she gave was out of love. And such love asks nothing in return."

The long lashes fluttered downward, but as if her weary brain had finally realized the impropriety of their intimate position, she struggled to keep herself awake.

"You should not be in here."

"No, but I do not intend to leave until you have fallen asleep," he informed her in firm tones.

"That is not necessary. I am not frightened of dreams."

"Close your eyes, Emma." He pressed her head upon the steady beat of his heart. "Tomorrow you can return to the intrepid Miss Cresswell. For tonight there is no need to be alone."

He thoroughly expected a struggle. The perverse minx could never accept that another might know what was best for her. Especially when that other was himself.

But astonishingly she did not pull away. Instead, she merely settled herself even closer as she lost her battle against the impending sleep.

With a wry smile Cedric shifted his head to place a kiss atop her head.

He did not know if it was the day's events or the dose of brandy that had caused her to be so uncharacteristically compliant, but he was thankful there was to be no argument.

For the moment, he was allowed to hold her tight in his arms, and that was all that mattered.

Twelve

Although it had been very late when Cedric at last left Emma sleeping peacefully and sought the comfort of his own bed, he was up in ample time to enjoy a brisk ride before returning to Mayford and the large breakfast awaiting.

Although he possessed a stiff neck from his hours of propping Emma upon his chest, he felt in remarkably good spirits as he devoured the mound of eggs and thick slice of ham Mrs. Borelli pressed upon him.

Strange, considering he was still concerned for his aunt and that the work on his gatehouse was being started without his supervision. He told himself that it must be the fact that the sun had decided to struggle its way through the gray clouds. It certainly made a pleasant change from the days of drizzling rain. But he knew that his light heart had far more to do with the scent of Emma that still lingered upon his skin.

It had been a wrench to leave her at all last night. Every instinct had urged him to pull the covers over them and remain locked together until the dawn beckoned. It was only the knowledge that not even the eccentric household of Mayford would tolerate such scandalous behavior that had at last forced him to slip from the bed.

Who imagined simply holding a woman in his arms could make the day seem a bit brighter?

Gads, he was becoming daft, he thought as he left the breakfast room and made his way to the library.

Although it was far too early to call upon his aunt, he had no doubt that when he did, she would be fussing to be allowed to rise. He hoped to forestall her demands with a selection of her favorite gothic novels.

He was busily piling the novels onto the Chippendale desk, when Mallory silently slid into the room and offered a half-bow.

"Pardon me, my lord, but a Mr. Winchell has called."

Cedric abandoned his work with a start of surprise. He had nearly forgotten the mysterious Mr. Winchell in the confusion of yesterday. Now he felt his curiosity once again stirred to life.

Clearly Emma was not about to confide the truth. Perhaps he would have better luck with the gentleman.

"Show him in, Mallory," he commanded, moving to stand in the center of the room.

"Very good."

Disappearing from the room, the butler returned in just moments with a lean gentleman attired in black.

At first glance it would be a simple matter to dismiss him as a modest, even dull fellow. Just the sort to run various errands for a proper bishop. But Cedric did not allow himself to be deceived by the clever image.

One only had to note the studied elegance of the man's movements and the natural hint of arrogance in his carriage to realize he was no man's toady.

Here was a gentleman more accustomed to giving orders than taking them.

There was no doubt, however, that the concern etched upon the thin face was genuine enough, Cedric acknowledged as the man hurried forward.

"My lord," he greeted with a hurried bow.

"Mr. Winchell."

"Forgive me for intruding, but I heard that there has

been an accident." He came directly to the point of his visit.

"My aunt has suffered a minor mishap," Cedric admitted, not willing to indulge the local gossips with details of his aunt's accident.

"Oh." Mr. Winchell gave a shake of his head. "I thought . . ."

"Yes?"

As if realizing that Cedric was closely scrutinizing his confusion, Mr. Winchell smoothly regained his composure.

Far too smoothly, Cedric told himself.

"I understood that there had been a fire and that Miss Cresswell was gravely injured."

Cedric grimaced. As usual, the local rattles had been busily spreading the latest rumors. And as usual, they paid scant attention to the truth.

"Miss Cresswell did acquire a few burns upon her hands," he conceded. "Thankfully, nothing that will not heal within a day or two."

Mr. Winchell briefly closed his eyes before opening them to smile in relief.

"Thank God."

"Thank God, indeed," Cedric agreed, sensing the older gentleman had been far more concerned than warranted by a causal acquaintance with Emma. "Will you have a seat? You appear rather undone."

With a faint nod of his head Mr. Winchell chose a wing chair beside the fire. Cedric moved to place himself in the matching chair. Close enough to study the guarded expression upon the lean countenance.

"I will admit that when I heard the rumors, I feared the worst." Mr. Winchell attempted to dismiss his concern with a shrug.

Cedric was not fooled for a moment. First there had been Emma's stricken reaction to this man's arrival in

Kent, and now his barely concealed panic at the fear Emma had been harmed. There was definitely a history between the two of them.

Now he just had to discover what that history was. And what his intentions were toward Emma.

Concern or no concern, Cedric would have the gentleman flogged and hauled out of Kent if he so much as brought a frown to her lovely face.

"You must be very close to Miss Cresswell to have become so concerned," he challenged with no attempt at subtlety.

His sudden attack brought a glint of mockery to the green eyes nearly hidden behind the thick glasses.

"Naturally, as an old friend of the family, I am concerned."

"More than an old friend, I suspect," Cedric charged.

He had hoped to disconcert the man. To catch him off guard and startle him into revealing his connection to Emma.

Instead, the older man lifted a practiced brow that would have effectively cowed a lesser gentleman.

No toady, indeed, Cedric acknowledged with a wry flicker of admiration.

"And I would suspect that you take more than a casual interest in your aunt's companion." He deflected the thrust with the skill of a worthy fencer. "I noted your tendency to hover around her like a hawk guarding his prey."

Cedric felt a swift stab of annoyance.

He did not particularly care to be likened to a hawk. And he liked even less that this stranger dared to comment on his possessive desire to protect Emma.

Then the annoyance faded as swiftly as it had arisen.

Good Lord, he had nearly allowed the overly clever man to lure him into his own trap. His cool words had been quite deliberate to goad him into an impetuous confession.

Of course, he thought with a hint of amusement, the gentleman could not be nearly so well acquainted with Emma as he supposed if he were willing to thrust her into the role of hapless prey.

Gads, she would shred a mere hawk to a mound of feathers with the sharp edge of her frigid composure.

"I consider her to be a friend," he informed his guest, allowing a distinct note of warning into his words. "And as a friend I would take deep offense to anyone who would wish to disturb her."

Mr. Winchell acknowledged the threat with a graceful nod of his head, a peculiar smile tugging at his mouth.

"I assure you that I have nothing but Emma's best interest at heart. It is high time she had a bit of happiness in her life."

Cedric was not so easily swayed. He could not forget the expression upon Emma's face when she had first caught sight of this gentleman. She clearly did not believe that this man possessed her best interest. Indeed, there had been more than a hint of fear lurking in her emerald gaze.

He slowly narrowed his eyes. "I could not agree more, which is why I feel it imperative to point out that your presence seems to bring more distress than joy to Emma."

A dangerous anger sharpened the older gentleman's features, causing Cedric a twinge of unease. He suddenly realized that this man could be a formidable enemy if he chose. There was something utterly ruthless in his countenance.

Then, in a blink of an eye, the anger disappeared and he gave a rueful grimace.

"Our past is not without its troubles," he said with an air of regret. "I tend to behave in a reckless fashion and have courted more scandal than any young maiden could hope to forgive. I intend the future to be far different."

Cedric did not miss the import of his words.

More scandal than any young maiden could hope to forgive . . .

Was this man the reason Emma was determined to close herself off from the world? And why she was willing to flee from those who cared for her to search for some unexplainable sense of security?

His hands curled into fists as he battled the urge to reach across and plant the man a facer.

"Why are you here?" he rasped.

If Mr. Winchell sensed Cedric's sudden desire to bloody his nose, he gave no indication as he gave a lift of one shoulder.

"That, my lord, is between Emma and myself."

Barely aware that he was moving, Cedric surged to his feet, his brows pulled together in a frown.

"If you hurt her—"

"I could say the same for you, Lord Hartshore," Mr. Winchell cut into his warning words, elegantly pushing himself out of his chair. "Emma is unlike most young ladies. She is unaccustomed to common flirtations and the delicious games played between men and women. She could easily mistake flattery for sincerity."

Cedric was taken aback by the sudden assault.

Did this man dare to imply that he was trifling with Emma's affections? Or, worse, that he was dastardly enough to lure an innocent maiden into a scandalous liaison?

Heavens above, Emma was more precious to him than his own life. He would fall upon Mrs. Borelli's cleaver before he would offer her insult.

"Emma will come to no harm through me," he said in tight tones.

"I pray you are right."

* * *

Emma was not certain what led her to the conservatory.

It was not until she stepped into the room and was surrounded by the warm scent of earth and pungent fragrance of flowers that she realized being here made her feel closer to Cedric.

A rueful smile tugged her lips as she settled upon a short bench.

When she had awoken that morning, she had tried to stir a sense of outrage at the memory of his presence in her bed. Good heavens, if someone had walked in on them, she would have been thoroughly compromised.

But despite her best efforts, she had been unable to find anything but gratitude within her. And astonishingly, a hint of regret that when she awoke she was no longer in Cedric's arms.

She had never felt so safe as she had with her head laid upon his chest. As if the world could not trouble her with Cedric at her side.

She gave a sharp shake of her head.

She had no right to such thoughts. Soon she would be leaving Kent. She would once again have no one to depend upon but herself.

Which was precisely what she wanted, was it not?

"What a lovely vision."

The smoky, dark voice sent a familiar tingle down her spine as Emma turned to watch Cedric strolling down the path toward her.

Her heart halted, then awkwardly surged back to life at the sight of his splendid form shown to advantage in the charcoal jacket and black breeches.

Gads, but he was handsome, she thought with a pang.

"Cedric."

"Do not tell me that you are a secret gardener?"

Emma briefly thought of the numerous plants and flowers she had effectively murdered over the years.

"No, I shall leave such talent to you."

The golden gaze swept over her upturned countenance with a near tangible force.

"How are you this morning?"

Feeling oddly vulnerable, Emma lowered her head.

"I am sorry that I disturbed you last night."

Although Emma did not glance up, she would have sworn he stroked a hand over her curls.

"I was not disturbed. You must know I delight in any excuse to be near you."

She shivered, the potent image of lying in his arms difficult to dismiss.

"I am not usually so silly as to be disturbed by a mere dream."

"No, you do not ever allow yourself to be silly," he said in dry tones. "It might be better if you did."

A small, uncomfortable silence fell, and with a determined effort Emma lifted her head to meet his searching gaze.

"Have you seen Lady Hartshore this morning?"

"No, not yet." He considered a moment before giving a shrug. "Actually, I just finished a rather interesting interview with Mr. Winchell."

Emma stiffened. Blast her father. Had she not made it clear she wanted him to stay far away from her?

"He is at Mayford?"

"He just took his leave."

She heaved a small sigh of relief. At least she would not have to face him so early in the day.

"Oh."

The golden gaze briefly flicked down to her clenched hands before returning to her wary expression.

"He came because he was quite concerned for you, my dear. He had heard rumors you were injured."

The mere notion of the Devilish Dandy being concerned for anyone made her lips thin.

"I hope you managed to reassure him that I am well?"

"After considerable effort. He was clearly shaken by the thought you had been injured."

"I find that difficult to believe," she muttered.

"He also issued what I can only presume to be a warning," he smoothly continued.

Emma frowned in bewilderment. "What?"

"He expressly informed me that you were an innocent and that I was not to trifle with your affections."

Emma felt a wave of embarrassment rush through her. What was Solomon thinking? He had never so much as noted her existence before, and now he was gadding about, playing the role of the domineering father as if he were determined to make up for twenty-three years of neglect in a few short weeks.

To even think he would warn away Lord Hartshore as if he were some common lecher . . . it did not even bear considering.

"I am sorry. I cannot imagine why he would do such a thing."

"Because he obviously realizes that you could easily have your heart broken," he said gently. "I assured him that was certainly not my intention."

"Of course not." With a jerky motion she rose to her feet and turned away. She supposed it was too much to hope the ground would open up and swallow her whole. "The mere notion is absurd."

"Yes, it is. I would never do anything to harm you." She heard him move to stand directly behind her, then without warning he grasped her shoulders to firmly turn her to face him. "Do you believe me, Emma?"

"Yes."

"Look at me."

She wanted to ignore his soft command. The sudden

tension that throbbed in the air warned her that the familiar awareness that always smoldered between them was threatening to blaze to life.

But a force beyond her control was suddenly in command of her body, and her head abruptly rose to reveal the excitement darkening her eyes.

"Emma," he breathed, his hands tightening on her shoulders as he tugged her against his hard body and claimed her mouth in a hungry kiss.

Emma felt a shock of pleasure run through her. Before, Cedric had always taken great care to keep his passions in check. His kisses had been a gentle exploration, coaxing her innocent desire with a slow insistence.

She felt as if she had been plunged into a raging ocean without warning. The lips that had coaxed now demanded, parting her own, and Cedric searched the sensitive skin of her inner mouth with his tongue.

A near unbearable heat pulsed through her blood as she clutched at his coat. She had not been prepared for the stark, aching need that was opening in the pit of her stomach.

She wanted him to drag her even closer.

To push her down among the flowers and . . .

Horrified by the vivid image of being laid down and covered by the large body, she abruptly pulled out of his grasp.

She was shameless.

Utterly, utterly shameless.

"Emma, forgive me," Cedric rasped, clearly misinterpreting her sudden rejection. "I did not mean to frighten you."

"You did not frighten me."

He reached out to grasp her chin, forcing her to meet his darkened gaze.

"Then, what is it?"

She could hardly confess that she had been overcome

by the desire to lie among the flowers and allow him to have his delicious way with her. Instead, she unconsciously pressed her tongue to her faintly swollen lips.

"I leave at the end of the week."

She was unprepared for the sudden anger that snapped his brows together.

"You still intend to leave Kent?"

"I . . . yes."

"May I ask why?"

She shifted uneasily, unaccustomed to this stern, demanding side of Cedric.

"I think it is for the best."

Her words only hardened his masculine features. "You cannot convince me that you are leaving because of Aunt Cassie. Even a fool could see that you are very much attached to her."

She pressed a hand to her stomach. "Please, I would rather not discuss this."

"No, you never wish to discuss anything, do you, Emma?" he charged. "It is so much easier to walk away than confront such untidy things as commitment and emotions."

She gasped at his attack. "That isn't fair."

"Does it not trouble you at all that my aunt will be devastated when you leave?"

The fact that it bothered her more than she wanted to admit made her meet his glittering gaze squarely.

"You are the one who insisted that I remain a month. I wanted to leave the day I arrived."

He flinched at her impetuous words, but before she could call them back, he was offering her a humorless smile.

"You are right. I have no one to blame but myself."

With a stiff bow he turned around to stride from the room.

Emma watched the uncompromising line of his body as he walked away, her heart clenching with an unbearable regret.

If only . . .

Thirteen

The Valentine ball was a stunning success.

Amid the lavish decorations that had transformed the ballroom into a mystical garden, the costumed guests mingled and flirted with an abandon that could be attributed either to the fanciful masks that hid their identities or the copious amount of champagne being distributed by the fairy-clad servants.

Stepping into the glittering scene, Cedric easily spotted his aunt attired in a frilly white gown with a crown upon her head that he supposed was meant to represent her role as queen of the fairies.

He allowed a small smile to touch his mouth. The first smile in nearly five long days.

Although his anger when he had stormed from Mayford had calmed over the past few days, he had remained restless and frustrated. Why was the contrary minx determined to abandon them? Why would she not confess what she was running from? Why would she kiss him with trembling passion and yet refuse to admit that there was something magical between them?

Why? Why? Why?

The questions had plagued him until he had at last determined that he could not allow her to walk away without one last attempt to prove she was making a terrible mistake.

And so he had sent a note to his aunt and attired himself in a ridiculous toga with laurel leaves in his dark hair before heading to Mayford.

Now he was eager to discover Emma so that he could speak with her alone.

Using his considerable height to scan the vast crowd, his search was abruptly interrupted as his aunt gave a cry of delight and hurried forward.

"Cedric, at last. How dashing you look."

Cedric widened his smile as he glanced down at the silk toga. "Yes, I thought it rather dashing myself."

Cassie leveled him a shrewd gaze. "Apollo, are you not?"

"How did you guess?" he demanded.

"I suspected your choice of costume when you sent me the note requesting that Emma come as Daphne. It was Apollo, was it not, who was struck by Eros' bow and fell hopelessly in love with the wood nymph?"

Cedric was uncertain what had prompted his impulsive desire to see Emma dressed as Daphne. Perhaps simply because the tragic tale so accurately reflected his own futile emotions.

"Yes."

Cassie's brow furrowed as she struggled to recall the sad tale.

"But did not Daphne repulse his advances and flee into the forest?"

His mouth twisted with wry humor. "Not only that, but she cried out to her father, the river god, to save her from Apollo's determined pursuit, and he promptly turned her into a laurel tree."

"Goodness, that is not very romantic," Cassie protested.

"But unfortunately quite appropriate."

She searched his dark features a moment before a sly smile curved her mouth.

"Do you seek to pursue Emma?"

A brief, disturbing memory of their passionate kiss in the conservatory rose to mind. Gads, he had not meant to lose control in such a fashion. He had intended to reassure her, nothing more. But the moment he touched her, he knew he was lost. The softness of her slender body, the flare of innocent desire in the emerald eyes, the pungent scent of flowers, all combined to send a rush of hungry need surging through his body.

He wanted her. Wanted her with a force he had never before experienced.

And he was not entirely certain that if she had not halted him he would not have taken her there and then.

He gave a shake of his head. "I fear that any such effort would be as futile as Apollo's quest."

"Yes, she does seem to be a bit skittish," Cassie agreed. "Perhaps it would be best to woo rather than pursue her."

Cedric felt his heart clench with an awful pain. "Wise words, no doubt, but my attempts to woo have proven to be singularly ineffective. And I no longer have the luxury of time."

"What shall you do?"

"I haven't the faintest notion."

An expression of sympathy settled on the birdlike features. "All will be well, my dear."

Cedric wished he possessed the same blithe ability to trust in fickle Fate. He far preferred to trust in his own efforts.

"Where is the minx?"

"I have her guarding the Valentine box." Cassie waved toward a distant corner. "And do not forget that you must draw a name and pin it to your sleeve. We shall remove them at midnight so that you can discover your true Valentine. Such fun, do you not think?"

Cedric barely heard his aunt's chatter as his gaze at

last caught sight of the woman who had haunted his thoughts for the past five days.

At first he did not even recognize her.

Gone was the spinster in her shapeless gray gown and tightly bound bun at the back of her head. In her place was a . . . temptress.

The gown in a green gauze with silver thread floated and sparkled around her slender form. Her golden hair had been left loose to flow past her shoulders with a crown of silver leaves encircling her head. Not even the green mask managed to distract from her stunning beauty.

"Good Lord," Cedric exclaimed, feeling as if the breath had been kicked from his body.

"Do you approve?" Cassie teased, easily reading his stunned expression.

"I am not sure." His startled gaze moved to the amazing amount of white skin exposed by the low-cut neckline. A stirring beneath his toga made him sternly rein in his wayward thoughts. "She will no doubt have every lecher in the room after her," he muttered.

"It is rather a charming costume."

He flashed her a speaking glance before plunging into the crowd with a determined expression. The only lecher who was going to be allowed close to Emma tonight was himself.

It took several exasperating minutes to force his way through the crush, but at last, physically shoving aside a slender gentleman attired as Cupid, he managed to halt next to Emma.

Busy pinning a slip of paper on the sleeve of a very round Romeo, she did not notice his approach until he leaned close to her and softly whispered in her ear.

" 'All but the nymph that should redress his wrong, attend his passion and approve his song.' "

"Cedric." She stepped back with an awkward motion, her expression wary.

Hardly surprising, he acknowledged, considering his ill humor during their last encounter.

"Apollo," he corrected her. "And you make a beautiful Daphne."

Her tongue peeked out to wet her lips, and Cedric once again was forced to still that stirring beneath his toga. Dash it all, he had been so very careful not to allow his gaze to stray to the temptation of that indecent neckline.

"I suppose you came over to draw a name?" she abruptly demanded, holding out the box until he reluctantly plucked a folded paper so she could pin it to the edge of his toga. "You cannot look at it until midnight."

"Unlike my aunt, I have no belief in such foolish superstition."

Her gaze tentatively lifted to his own. "No?"

"No," he said huskily. "I have no need to pin a lady's name to my sleeve to know that she has found a place in my heart."

The emerald eyes widened at the unmistakable meaning in his words, but with her usual perverse manner she hastily attempted to divert him.

"Your aunt must be pleased with such a turnout. I believe that everyone who received an invitation must be here."

"Cassie is a great favorite among the neighborhood."

"Yes."

Not about to waste the evening with banal chatter, Cedric stepped closer.

"Dance with me, Emma."

She gave an anxious shake of her head. "I do not care much for dancing, I fear."

"Perhaps because you have not had the proper partner." Reaching out to firmly grasp her hand, he placed it on his arm and tugged her toward the couples preparing for the next dance.

Within moments they were moving in the familiar patterns. "This is not so horrid, is it?" he demanded as they came together.

"I feel as if everyone is staring at me," she muttered.

His lips twisted, well aware that at least every male was staring. How could they not?

"Of course they are, my dear," he forced himself to say in light tones. "You are very beautiful."

She gave a sudden frown. "I am not beautiful."

"I will agree that you try to hide your beauty behind those hideous gray gowns," he admitted. "But tonight you are . . . breathtaking."

A hint of color stained her cheeks as she hastily glanced toward the nearby dancers.

"You should not say such things. What if someone were to overhear you?"

Cedric merely smiled as he edged her toward the mingling crowd, then suddenly tugged her toward a nearby alcove.

"You are perfectly correct, my dear. We need to be somewhere that we can be alone."

Startled by his unexpected maneuver, Emma allowed herself to be led unresisting past the guests and even through the darkness of the alcove to the door that led to the garden.

It was not until they were actually upon the terrace that she belatedly dug in her heels.

"What are you doing?"

Glancing down at her delicate face, Cedric felt his heart lurch. With a smooth motion he tore off his mask and reached out to remove Emma's from her lovely countenance. He dropped them to the terrace without concern for their safety.

"This is where you belong, my Daphne," he whispered. "Among the shadows and silver moonlight."

She shivered, although he did not think it was entirely due to the crisp air.

"Lady Hartshore will wonder where we have gone."

With commendable restraint Cedric resisted the urge to trace the fine lines of her countenance. Her beauty was astonishingly luminous in the silver light.

"She is far too occupied to notice we are missing."

"Still, I should be at hand in case she is in need of me."

He strategically moved to block her path to the ballroom. This might be his last opportunity to speak with her alone. He was determined to have his say.

"My aunt will have to accustom herself to being without your services," he pointed out in low tones.

She flinched, her gaze abruptly lowering. "Yes, I suppose."

"Have you packed your bags?"

"Yes."

He drew in a steadying breath, wanting nothing more than to toss her over his shoulder and lock her in the nearest dungeon.

"And you received my bank draft?"

"Yes," she breathed so low, he could barely hear the word.

"So there is nothing left to keep you in Kent."

Her hands fluttered to press to her stomach. "I wish you would not make this more difficult."

Difficult? She thought he was making the situation difficult? Bloody hell. She was the one who was keeping barriers between them. Who refused to admit the attraction between them. Who was more determined to keep her secrets than open her heart to those who wished to love her.

"Unlike you, Emma, I cannot hide from my emotions.

I cannot pretend that it does not matter if you stay or leave."

She held out her hand. "No, please."

"Stay, Emma," he ground out, moving to grasp her shoulders in a tight grip. "Stay with me."

Her gaze flew upward, wide with distress. "I cannot."

"Cannot or will not?"

"Surely it amounts to the same thing?"

It did, of course, but the knowledge did nothing to ease the pain lancing through his body.

"At least tell me why, Emma. I deserve an explanation."

Just for a moment her lips parted, as if half of her wished to confess the truth. Then she was giving a sharp shake of her head.

"I cannot."

"Emma . . . if you are in trouble, you have only to tell me. Together we can face anything."

Her body trembled beneath his hands. "Not this."

A sharp flare of anger raced through his body. "Dammit, Emma, I cannot help if you will not trust me," he growled. "Tell me."

"No." She gave a wild shake of her head. "I cannot."

"Emma."

He was uncertain what he intended to say, but in the end it did not matter as she abruptly jerked from his grasp, and before he could halt her, she had raced across the terrace and disappeared into the shadows of the garden.

Closing his eyes, Cedric cursed his clumsy handling of the situation, the proprieties that insisted he did not chase after her into the dark garden, and most of all the vexing minx who was threatening to drive him to Bedlam.

Dammit all.

* * *

Emma knew she was behaving like a frightened child. Mature, sensible ladies did not bolt into dark gardens in the midst of a Valentine ball.

But at the moment she did not feel mature or particularly sensible.

She felt as if her heart were being slowly crushed by some brutal force.

Dear Lord, how tempted she had been to confess the truth. To reveal that she was the daughter of the Devilish Dandy and that her father was currently pretending to be Mr. Winchell.

She had no doubt that he would have pulled her into his arms and assured her that it made no difference to him. His heart was too noble, too true to be altered by whatever she might confess.

And that was precisely the problem, she acknowledged with a choked sob.

How could she possibly allow him to shoulder the scandal of the Devilish Dandy?

It was one thing to have an aunt who chatted with ghosts and an uncle who paraded around like a pirate. It was quite another to take on a notorious thief who might even now be clearing Hartshore Park of its finer works of art.

No. He was too good a man to taint with such shame. And more important she cared too deeply to allow him to make such a sacrifice.

She shivered as the icy breeze swirled around her. As much as she might long to remain hidden in the silent garden, she knew she would swiftly freeze.

Besides, whatever Cedric's words to the contrary, she was well aware Lady Hartshore would be expecting her to be at her side.

Moving back toward the terrace, she caught the faint whiff of a cheroot, then, as she neared the steps, she realized that two gentlemen were leaning against the stone railing.

She paused, debating whether to slip to a side door or risk the suspicion of arriving unescorted from the garden, when the sound of their voices floated downward.

"Are you certain?" a flamboyantly attired Casanova demanded.

"Of course I am certain," a heavyset Caesar retorted. "I heard it from the magistrate only a few moments ago."

"Well, if he believes the man to be the Devilish Dandy, then why the deuce does he not simply capture him?"

Emma clamped a hand over her mouth to keep herself from crying out in dismay. Dear heavens, it was what she had feared above all else. Somehow her father had been recognized.

"Because he cannot be certain," Caesar was continuing, thankfully unaware of the slender woman shivering in the shadows. "He has only the word of Lady Mosley, who swears he is the same gentleman who visited twenty years ago and made off with her rubies."

"That old tabbie?" Casanova gave a loud snort. "Fah, she would claim that her chef was Napoleon if she thought it would gain her a bit of notoriety."

"True enough, which is why Malton has sent to London for a Runner who has actually seen the Dandy. If it is a bust, then no harm done and the poor sod will never know he was fingered as a thief. If it is him, then he shall soon be receiving his just rewards."

Emma's thoughts were racing as she wrapped her arms around her frozen form.

They were not yet certain, she acknowledged numbly. They had only the vague memories of a woman prone to exaggerate the most trifling incident. Which meant that her father had until the Runner arrived to disappear from Kent.

"I'll wager it's a bust," Casanova scoffed. "What would a gent like the Devilish Dandy be doing in Kent?"

"Lady Hartshore possesses some fine jewels, and you won't find a better collection of art than at Hartshore Park."

"Mayhap, but hardly to the taste of the Devilish Dandy. It was said he returned a diamond tiara he had stolen from Lady Dunwell with a note that claimed the stones were of such an inferior quality that he feared Lord Dunwell must be a wretched skinflint and he could not possibly in good conscience steal her paltry baubles. She was so humiliated, she fled to the country until Lord Dunwell agreed to provide her with a decent set of jewels."

"Still, it would make a rousing good story if it were him," Caesar mused, clearly hoping the famous thief was lurking among them. "Just think of strolling into White's with the information we brushed elbows with the Devilish Dandy."

Emma felt a sick distaste roll through her stomach at the man's vain desire to see a man hang so he could impress the members of his club.

Casanova, however, was clearly struck by the notion of creating such a dash among his peers.

"That would make them blighters sit up and take notice. Can't abide their manner of staring down their London noses as if we smell of the country."

"Remember Wilford? He was practically mobbed when it was learned he had been standing next to the Dandy when he was arrested."

Emma had endured enough of their preening delight in the thought of using her father's capture to better their standing among the London snobs. Besides, she had no notion when the magistrate had sent for the Runner. For all she knew, he might even now be racing his way to

Kent. She had to act swiftly if she were to save her father from certain death.

Moving as silently as her stiff limbs would allow, she backed away from the terrace, then skirting the house, she hurried to a side door that would allow her to enter unnoted.

She had not seen her father arrive at the ball, but she knew beyond a doubt that the ambitious vicar would never miss the social event of the year. He would also insist Mr. Winchell be close at hand to view his privileged status among the fashionable families.

Entering the house, she took a moment to allow the welcome warmth to unthaw her trembling body before hurrying down the long corridor toward the ballroom.

The sound of music and laughter echoed through the air long before she reached the doors of the ballroom. But even as her steps picked up speed, a large, decidedly male form abruptly detached itself from the shadows along the wall.

Unprepared for the sudden obstruction in her path, Emma was unable to halt in time to avoid crashing into the solid body.

She reeled backward, but before she could fall, a pair of strong arms encircled her waist and pulled her upright.

"Emma," a familiar male voice muttered in exasperation.

Glancing into Cedric's dark features, Emma forgot she was deeply dreading encountering this gentleman after their earlier argument. For the moment she could think of nothing beyond the danger to her father.

"Cedric, have you seen Mr. Winchell?"

His brows lowered at her odd question, clearly sensing the tremors that still raced through her form.

"Not to my knowledge, but this is a masquerade. He could be one of any number of Romeos and Samsons around."

"I must find him," she breathed, too upset to hide the fear that raced through her blood.

The golden eyes narrowed at the hectic flush that stained her countenance.

"Why?"

"I cannot explain now."

At her hurried words, the male features hardened in exasperation.

"Enough of this," he growled, abruptly hauling her off her feet and marching into a nearby room that had been set aside to house the cloaks and hats of the guests. Slamming shut the door, he set her down on her feet and glared into her desperate countenance.

"No, Cedric. I must find my . . . Mr. Winchell."

She attempted to step past his looming form, but his hands reached out to grasp her shoulders.

"You are going nowhere until you tell me precisely what is going on."

"I do not have time—"

"On the contrary," he sharply cut into her words, his expression warning her that he was in no humor to be ignored. "You have all the time in the world. We are not leaving this room until you have told me precisely what has occurred."

Fourteen

Cedric realized he was handling the situation badly.

He had no right to hold this woman hostage and force her to confess secrets she preferred to keep hidden.

But the sight of her stricken expression and the unmistakable trembling of her slender body had snapped the thin thread of his patience.

Blast it all, something terrible had clearly occurred to upset her, and he could not meekly stand aside and allow her to face it alone.

Even if it meant using his superior strength to induce her to confide the truth.

Glaring at him in exasperation, she gave a shake of her head.

"You do not understand."

"That much I readily agree with," he retorted, his voice as harsh as his expression. "Explain."

Even in the dim candlelight he could make out the play of emotions that crossed her countenance. Anger, impatience, and, at last, resignation at the knowledge he was fully determined to keep her trapped in the room until she confessed.

"Mr. Winchell is in danger," she finally admitted in tight tones.

"Danger?" His brows snapped together in surprise. This was not at all what he had expected. "From what?"

She drew in a shaky breath. "I overheard two of the guests speaking in the garden. The magistrate has sent for a Runner to capture him."

Familiar with the plodding but thorough magistrate, Cedric was certain he would never have contacted London for a Runner without good cause.

"Why the devil would the magistrate be interested in Mr. Winchell?"

"Because he is not Mr. Winchell. He is the Devilish Dandy."

Cedric's hands unconsciously tightened as his eyes widened in shock. Despite the fact he spent the majority of his life in the wilds of Kent, even he had heard of the Devilish Dandy. Gads, who had not been entertained by tales of his daring capers and dashing style?

"The jewel thief," he muttered, unable to reconcile the somber Mr. Winchell with the rumors of the satin-attired, sharp-witted fop.

"Yes."

"Good Lord." A sudden, wholly unwelcome realization struck him. "You knew who he was."

She gave a slow, reluctant nod of her head. "Yes."

"How?"

She was silent for so long, Cedric feared she might refuse to answer him. Then, tugging out of his grasp, she turned to hide her troubled expression.

"He is my father."

At first he thought he must have misunderstood her whispered words.

She was the daughter of the Devilish Dandy?

Nonsense.

Surely any such daughter would be a hardened criminal just like her father? Or at least a forward hussy who was willing to use any trick or wile to seduce the unwary?

Not this cool, controlled lady who cherished propriety above all things.

Then the truth hit him like a kick in the head.

Of course.

It all made sense.

The priceless emerald around her neck. Her determined flight to Kent. Her unreasonable fear of any hint of scandal. Her refusal to allow anyone close to her. And, of course, her reaction to the arrival of Mr. Winchell.

She might be the daughter of the Devilish Dandy, but she was desperate to rid herself of his legacy. Even if it meant a lifetime of loneliness.

"What is he doing here?" he asked softly.

A shudder raced through her body. "He came to offer me an allowance so that I would no longer be forced to earn my living."

Whatever his distaste for a gentleman who would steal from others, he had to approve of his desire to help his daughter. Even if his offer was clearly luring Emma away from Kent.

"So that is why you are leaving."

"No." She jerkily spun to face him, her eyes glittering in the candlelight. "I want nothing from him. Not ever."

She could not disguise the raw edge in her voice, and Cedric stepped toward her.

"He has hurt you."

She gave a sharp, humorless laugh. "I assure you that there is nothing pleasant about being the daughter of the Devilish Dandy."

Cedric could readily imagine. Although the speculation and twitters that were directed toward his aunt were slight indeed when compared to those aimed at the Devilish Dandy, he knew how unpleasant such rumors could be.

"He is the reason you came to Kent."

She wrapped her arms around her waist in an unconsciously defensive motion.

"I could bear the scandal no longer."

"And then you arrived at Mayford." His lips twisted in rueful amusement. "No wonder you were so horrified."

"I wanted only to find a place where I could fade into obscurity."

Cedric's heart rebelled at the mere notion. This lovely, kind, courageous woman fade into obscurity? No. It would be a sin against nature.

She was meant to love and laugh and enjoy the sheer wonder of life.

She was meant to be at his side, in his bed, and holding their children in her arms.

And that was precisely what he intended to see happen.

"You were trying to hide," he said softly.

"Perhaps."

"That is never possible, my dear. The truth invariably finds us."

He was startled when the magnificent emerald eyes flooded with tears.

"So I have discovered."

"Oh, Emma, do not cry," he whispered, unable to halt himself from reaching out and pulling her into his arms. "All will be well." He echoed his aunt's familiar saying.

She pressed her face against his chest, battling her tears. "No, it will never be well. Not ever."

Careful not to startle her, Cedric lifted his hand to gently cup her chin and press it upward.

"Trust me," he said in firm tones. "Can you do that, Emma?"

She gazed at him for a moment before giving a nod of her head.

"Yes."

"Good girl." He bent down to brush his lips softly over her forehead before stepping back. He wanted nothing more than to remain locked in the room with Emma in his arms, but he realized that such a pleasurable activity would have to wait. Whatever her strained relationship with her father, it was obvious she was terrified that he was about to be captured. Right or wrong, he was going to do everything in his power to ensure that did not occur. With an unconscious frown he sifted through a variety of schemes before he at last hit upon the one that would pose the least danger to Emma. "I want you to return to the ballroom and find your father. Bring him to the stables as soon as possible."

She gnawed her bottom lip until he feared she might draw blood.

"But the magistrate is certain to have him followed. He would not wish to miss an opportunity to capture the Devilish Dandy."

"I have thought of that," he assured her.

"What will you do?"

"Trust me," he said gently.

With a wavering smile she slipped past him and pulled open the door, then, without warning, she abruptly turned back to regard him with a searching gaze.

"Why are you doing this?"

Cedric did not even have to consider his answer. Although it had taken him some time to accept the truth, he had no doubt precisely why he was willing to move heaven and earth to make this woman happy.

"Because I love you."

She gave a slow shake of her head. "But my father . . ."

"I do not care if your father is the Devilish Dandy, Napoleon, or the King of England. We are in this together, Emma." He battled yet another urge to pull her into his arms and prove once and for all the depths of his love. "Now go."

She regarded him for another moment before slipping through the door and disappearing into the shadows.

Once alone, Cedric heaved a sigh.

That was not at all how he intended to confess his love. He had wanted the romance of the garden, the soft shimmer of moonlight, and Emma in his arms.

But she had refused to hear his pleas of love in the garden, and then the debacle of her father ruined any further opportunity to be alone with Emma tonight.

He would make it up to her, he silently promised. In the morning he would make a proper call to Mayford complete with flowers and his mother's diamond ring. Perhaps not as romantic as he would wish, but certainly drenched in all the respectability she could desire.

Unable to halt the foolish smile that tugged at his lips, Cedric left the room and headed deeper into the house. He had to find his groom before Emma arrived in the stables.

I love you. . . .

The three simple words spun through Emma's mind as she entered the ballroom and began the anxious task of locating her father.

Never could she have dreamed that such an honorable, wonderful gentleman would fall in love with her. How could she? Her connection with the Devilish Dandy alone was enough to ensure that most gentlemen would never consider her a lady. And she certainly did not possess the beauty to tempt a man to overlook her scandalous relative.

But Cedric . . .

A fierce pain clutched at her heart. He could have any

woman he chose. What lady could possibly resist his ready charm, his masculine beauty, and his kind heart?

He deserved a wife who would bring pride to his name, who would walk down the streets of London with her head held high, and be at his side when he entertained his friends.

How could she allow him to sacrifice all he deserved for her?

The answer, of course, was that she couldn't.

She swayed at the sharp-edged regret that raced through her body. Dear heavens, she was trying to do what was right. How could it hurt so badly?

Suddenly catching sight of a flamboyantly attired Don Juan, Emma thrust aside her dark thoughts. Now was not the time to brood upon the painful irony of fate. She had to warn her father before it was too late.

Halting at his side, Emma impatiently waited for him to perform an elegant bow.

"Ah, Emma." He glanced over her absurd costume. "Daphne, I presume?"

She ignored his teasing as she tightly grasped his arm. "You must come with me."

He frowned as he reached up to slip off his mask. "Is something the matter?"

With a hasty glance around to ensure there was no one near, she leaned closer.

"You have been recognized."

"I see." He smiled wryly as he held out his arm. "Shall we dance?"

She frowned at his blithe dismissal of his danger. "Did you hear me? The magistrate has been warned that you are the Devilish Dandy."

"And if we rush from the room, even the most dim-witted magistrate would be certain I am," he pointed out gently. "Come along."

With a shivering reluctance Emma allowed herself to

be led onto the floor, relieved to discover more than a few guests had already tossed aside their masks. At least they would not attract undue interest, she assured herself.

"You are appearing quite beautiful this evening, Emma," her father murmured as they waltzed toward the far side of the room.

"I wish to goodness that I had insisted I remain in my chambers," she muttered.

He twirled her toward the edge of the floor. "You cannot hide forever, Emma."

She flashed him an exasperated frown. "I will not have this conversation now, Father."

"Very well." He shrugged, then, with the same skill Cedric had earlier employed, he smoothly steered them off the floor and through a side door. Following his lead, Emma briefly wondered if all men learned how to slip a lady from a crowded room. It was certainly a convenient if disreputable talent to possess.

Gathering her composure, she took charge of the situation. "We will use the servants' entrance," she warned him swiftly, leading them away from the glittering ballroom.

They silently moved through the dark halls toward the back of the house. Thankfully the entire household was busy helping with the numerous guests, and they were easily able to avoid the handful of distracted footmen.

Emma heaved a sigh of relief as they at last reached the back door, but even as she prepared to pull it open, her father laid a hand upon her shoulder.

"Just a moment, Emma."

She glanced over her shoulder with a hint of impatience. Surely her father could not comprehend the danger he was in.

"We must hurry," she insisted.

"Not until you tell me something."

"What?"

"Why are you helping me?" he demanded, his green eyes glittering in the dim light. "You could have allowed the magistrate to capture me and you would have been rid of me forever."

Emma could not halt her startled gasp. "You believe I would wish you dead?" she whispered in shock.

He shrugged. "It would be a sure means of ending the scandal I carry with me."

An ugly wave of guilt rushed through her. It was true she had always resented the scandal her father had brought down upon them. And even that she had desired to punish him for the pain she had suffered. Was that not why she had refused the money he had offered?

But never, never would she desire to see him hauled to the gallows.

He was her father. And whether she occasionally forgot the fact for her self-pity, she loved him.

"No," she breathed, reaching out to lightly touch his face. "I have never wished harm upon you."

"I am glad to know that." He reached up to grasp her hand and pressed it to his lips.

They remained like that for a moment, then, realizing that they were wasting valuable time, she tugged her hand free.

"Come, we must go."

With as much caution as possible they left the house and made their way to the distant stables. Even then Emma motioned for her father to remain in the shadows until she ensured there was no Runner waiting to trap him. Waving him forward, she hesitantly moved toward the back of the stalls.

"Cedric?" she called softly

On cue the tall, impossibly handsome gentleman stepped from the shadows.

"I am here, Emma." He offered a faint bow toward her companion. "Mr. Cresswell."

Solomon offered his own lavish bow. "My lord."

Moving forward, Cedric regarded the older gentleman in a stern manner.

"I believe we can safely presume that the magistrate has ensured the house is being watched." He came straight to the point.

Solomon gave a nod. "If he possesses any sense."

"Then we shall have to provide a diversion."

"Do you have a plan?"

"Yes." Cedric lifted his hand, and a thin, tall man attired in livery stepped forward. "I want you to exchange clothes with my groom. He will take your mount and ride toward London. I have given him orders not to halt under any circumstances until he reaches a small inn at Rakeshore, where he is to take a room and remain there until I send word he can return."

"So the magistrate's men will believe me holed up at the inn while I slip away," the Devilish Dandy said slowly.

"Precisely. You will become my groom, and once we reach Hartshore Park you will be able to leave unnoted."

An unmistakable gleam of appreciation entered the green eyes. "I must commend you upon your swift wits, my lord."

Unimpressed by the highest praise the Devilish Dandy could offer a gentleman, Cedric met his gaze squarely.

"I do this for Emma."

Surprisingly, Solomon smiled broadly at the stern warning. "I did not doubt that for a moment."

Cedric gave a grunt, then abruptly reached out to drop a leather bag in Solomon's hand.

"Here. There is enough money to allow you to return to London."

Solomon gave another bow. "I shall repay you within the month."

Cedric waved a dismissive hand. "There is no need."

"Thank you." The Devilish Dandy turned toward his silent daughter. "You will take care of Emma for me?"

"I intend to do my very best," Cedric promised in a low voice.

"Then I leave her in good hands." He reached out to softly brush Emma's cheek. "Emma, if you have need of me, you have only to write Rachel. I shall come in an instant."

An unexpected warmth flooded her heart. Certainly their relationship had always been troubled. And she did not doubt that their future would produce its share of conflict. But for now she felt as close to him as she ever had.

"Yes."

"And no more hiding," he chided her. "It is time to face your fears and allow yourself to find joy."

She bit her lower lip as the absurd tears once again threatened. There would be no joy once she left Kent. There would be nothing but the loneliness she had chosen.

"You must go," she forced herself to mutter.

"Au revoir, my dearest."

With a last smile the Devilish Dandy slipped toward the back of the stables along with the groom. Perhaps ridiculously, she sent up a prayer that he would be safe. She did not know if God looked over jewel thieves, but it could not hurt to try.

"Emma, we must return to the ballroom to avert suspicion," Cedric intruded upon her anxious thoughts, reaching out to place her hand upon his arm.

She heaved a faint sigh. The last thing she desired was to return to the hot, stuffy room and chatter aimlessly with complete strangers. Especially when she would be consumed with worry that her father had been discovered or the poor groom somehow injured during his daring ride toward London.

Still, she was aware that their prolonged absence was bound to arouse suspicion. And not only by the men watching the house for the magistrate.

"Yes."

Leading her out of the stables and across the yard, he glanced down at her pale countenance.

"I know it will be difficult, my dear, but I fear I must insist that you conjure a smile. I would not wish the guests to think that a short stroll upon my arm induces a fit of the sullens in a maiden."

She abruptly lifted her gaze, her expression troubled. "What if your groom is caught? Or they shoot him, thinking he is my father?"

He patted her hand in a comforting fashion. "Do not fear. My groom is a man of great resourcefulness. He will not be caught."

"I hope you are right," she muttered as he angled directly for the terrace.

"Do you not recall?" he teased lightly. "My aunt has already informed you that I am always right. It is my most annoying fault. Now, come, I believe they are playing a waltz."

Emma went.

From the terrace to the ballroom and into his arms.

She closed her eyes as they twirled across the floor, drinking in the feel and scent of the man who had firmly lodged himself into her heart.

For the moment her father was forgotten as she attempted to store a lifetime of memories in the one, all too short waltz.

Fifteen

Nearly a week later Emma lay upon a brocade-covered sofa with a lavender-scented cloth pressed to her aching forehead.

She was miserable.

No, worse than miserable.

Since the morning after the Valentine ball, when she had begged Lady Hartshore for a coach to take her to Lord Chance's estate, she had felt as if she were slowly dying. Not even being reunited with her beloved sister, Sarah, nor the warm welcome offered by Lord Chance, had managed to ease the pain tearing at her heart.

In truth, the constant sight of Sarah and Chance mooning over each other only reminded her of what she had lost.

It was not that she wasn't utterly delighted with her sister's good fortune, she was always swift to reassure herself. Or that she in any way disapproved of Lord Chance. How could she? He was perfect in every way.

But the sight of them together, holding hands, whispering in each other's ears, sharing glances that practically set the very air on fire, only underlined her loss.

Pressing the cloth even tighter, she fought back the urge to cry yet again. Gads, she had cried enough for a lifetime. And what had that achieved beyond a raging headache and running nose?

She should be concentrating on the future. Making plans for leaving Kent and returning to London. After all, she could not remain with Sarah forever. And since she had refused to take the salary Cedric had sent to Mayford, it was imperative that she find employment as swiftly as possible.

Unfortunately the mere thought of packing her bags and enduring the tedious carriage ride back to London made her headache worse.

A faint moan escaped her lips as the door to the dainty parlor was thrown open and Sarah strode firmly across the room to gaze down upon her.

As always, she appeared annoyingly beautiful in a rose satin gown, her hair artfully arranged, and her blue eyes shining with a deep sense of contentment. Her well-groomed loveliness only managed to make Emma feel sadly bedraggled in her gray gown and her features reddened by bouts of tears.

"Very affecting, my dear," her older sister drawled.

Startled by the strange words, Emma slowly lowered the cloth and met Sarah's narrowed gaze.

"Excuse me?"

The sympathy her sister had displayed since her unexpected arrival on her doorstep was distinctly absent as she studied the reclined form draped upon the sofa.

"I do not believe even the great Mrs. Siddons could capture the role of the tragic heroine with such dramatic flair."

Her headache forgotten Emma abruptly swung her feet to the floor and sat upright.

"What is that supposed to mean?"

Sarah shrugged. "I am merely expressing my appreciation for your lovely performance over the past week. All those heavy sighs, your refusal to do more than nibble at the chef's enticing creations, your pale countenance, and those wounded shadows beneath your eyes."

Emma could not have been more shocked if Sarah had entered the room and slapped her across the face. She could not imagine what had gotten into her sister.

"You believe me to be acting?" she demanded in confusion.

The blue eyes, as brilliant as the sapphire that hung around her neck, briefly darkened, but her expression remained set in lines of determination.

"No, but I do believe you are indulging in the most annoying bout of self-pity that it has ever been my misfortune to view."

Emma clenched her hands as she glared at the woman hovering over her. What had happened to the solicitous sister who had tucked her into bed each evening with a cup of hot chocolate?

"Perhaps you would prefer that I leave?" Emma retorted in stiff tones.

Expecting remorse, Emma was dumbfounded when Sarah gave an impatient click of her tongue.

"Oh, for goodness' sake, do not add being a martyr to your repertoire."

A surge of anger rushed through Emma at her sister's tart insult. Good heavens, how had she ever thought this woman the sweetest, kindest person in all of England?

"Forgive me for being a trifle upset at nearly watching my father being once again hauled to the gallows."

"Fah," Sarah scoffed. "That is not the reason you are moping around like some lost waif."

"How could you possibly know?" Emma demanded.

"Because I have seen that precise expression before."

Emma felt a trickle of unease inch down her spine. "Indeed?"

"Yes. I saw it in the mirror when I convinced myself Chance could not possibly love the daughter of the Devilish Dandy."

Emma shakily surged to her feet, unprepared for Sarah's shrewd perception.

She had deliberately not revealed her reason for leaving Mayford, instead implying it had been her father's near capture that had made it impossible for her to remain. She did not want Sarah's pity for being ridiculous enough to fall in love with a gentleman who deserved so much better than herself.

"Lord Chance is a very unique gentleman," she pointed out, well aware that Lord Chance was commonly referred to as the Flawless Earl. The staunch respectability of his family, not to mention himself, would protect them from any vicious gossip. Gads, he could no doubt marry Josephine without raising a brow.

"Well, I must, of course, agree, but he is not the only gentleman who would be willing to overlook such a connection for a woman he loved."

Emma attempted to appear unconcerned. "Perhaps."

Sarah was not fooled for a moment. Like a hound who had caught the scent of the fox, she was determined to corner her quarry.

"Did you not tell me that Lord Hartshore helped to hide Father from the magistrate?"

"I . . . yes."

"Odd." Sarah slowly smiled. "It would have been so much simpler to turn him over to the authorities. Think of the scandal had he been caught."

A familiar pain clutched at her heart at the mention of Cedric, and she briefly closed her eyes.

"Lord Hartshore pays little heed to the threat of scandal."

"He sounds perfect," Sarah announced in satisfied tones.

Emma wrenched her eyes open. Lud, could her sister not leave her in peace? She had no desire to dredge through her painful memories.

"Yes," she agreed in harsh tones. "He also bears an aunt who speaks with ghosts and her brother, who believes himself to be a pirate, not to mention a cook who tells fortunes. How could I ask him to take a wife who is the daughter of a wanted criminal?"

Sarah arched her brows. "Surely that is his decision to make?"

Emma heaved a frustrated sigh, giving a shake of her head. "He would not be sensible."

Astonishingly Sarah tilted back her head to give a tinkling laugh. "My dearest Emma, love is not meant to be sensible."

"One of us must be," Emma argued stubbornly.

Sarah stepped closer, her gaze closely examining the pale lines of her sister's countenance.

"You know, I am beginning to believe that you are fooling yourself, Emma."

"And what precisely is that supposed to mean?"

"I think you are afraid."

Emma stiffened at the ridiculous accusation. Afraid? Fah.

"That is absurd."

"No, it isn't," Sarah insisted, her expression suddenly softening. "Ever since Father's identity was revealed, you have done your best to fade from the world. First as a governess for the Falwells and then as a companion to Lady Hartshore."

"It is hardly shocking that I would wish to avoid any connection to the Devilish Dandy," she retorted, more than a little offended at being branded a coward.

Hadn't she refused any offers of help and supported herself? Hadn't she saved Lady Hartshore from the fire? Hadn't she helped her father escape from the magistrate?

Hardly the actions of a coward.

Sarah, however, seemed far less convinced of her heroic nature.

"No, but you have not been hiding from Father, you have been hiding from yourself," she accused Emma in soft tones. "And you know that to become the Countess of Hartshore means you have to face the world and admit the truth. That you are Emma Cresswell, daughter of the Devilish Dandy."

Emma took a step backward, her stomach heaving in an unpleasant fashion.

"No."

"Yes." Sarah relentlessly refused to be denied her say. "It is difficult, I know. I was terrified at the thought of announcing my engagement. I was accustomed to being with those who already knew who I was and accepted me. Suddenly I had to face Chance's family, his friends . . . I knew they might very well turn their backs on me."

With a small cry Emma abruptly turned around. Was it true? Could she have attempted to hide her own weak fears behind the noble cause of saving Cedric from scandal?

Her stomach heaved again, and she battled to keep herself from being sick all over the floral carpet.

She had been so certain she was doing what was best for Cedric. That her flight from Mayford would give him the opportunity to discover a proper maiden to be his wife. One who would bring with her a spotless reputation.

Now Sarah was ruthlessly forcing her to face the notion that her motives had been utterly selfish.

The image of Cedric's dark, handsome countenance rose to her mind. She shuddered at the thought of never seeing him again. Of spending the rest of her life as a dreary servant in some dreary household. Of dreaming night after lonely night of a pair of warm golden eyes and sweet roses.

"What have I done?" she whispered in a shaky voice.

Sarah moved to place a gentle hand upon her shoulder.

"Nothing that cannot be undone. Go back to Lord Hartshore. Tell him that you love him."

This time Emma did not even attempt to deny that the chill that raced through her was anything but pure fear.

"What if it's too late? What if he cannot forgive me for running away?"

"Then you will at least know that you tried," Sarah told her firmly. "Surely that is better than a lifetime of regret?"

Emma suddenly wiped away the tears that were freely running down her face.

"Yes."

The current Earl of Hartshore was in a foul mood.

Not an unusual occurrence over the past fortnight.

Since arriving at Mayford like a lovesick fool, only to discover that his intended had fled at the break of dawn, he had gnashed his teeth and stormed around Hartshore Park like a caged lion.

Egads, had there ever been a greater simpleton?

He had thought it was fear that made Emma keep him at a distance. That once he managed to uncover her secrets, she would welcome his love with open arms.

A humorless smile twisted his lips as he entered the library and headed directly for the decanter of brandy.

Obviously that had not been the case at all.

Not only was she not welcoming him with open arms, she had bolted rather than be embarrassed by his intended proposal.

And to add exquisite insult to injury, she had left behind her rightful salary.

As if she could not bear to accept a single thing from him.

He cursed beneath his breath, pouring a healthy measure of brandy and swallowing it in one gulp.

Reaching to once again fill his glass, his attention was suddenly captured by an ivory sheet of paper propped upon the mantel.

With a puzzled frown he crossed to pluck the note from its resting place and read the brief words sprawled across the parchment: *Meet me in the woods. Five o'clock.*

"What the blazes?" Striding to the corridor, he bellowed for his butler. "Winters."

With commendable speed the efficient butler appeared in the doorway, his expression holding a hint of surprise at the imperious summons.

"Yes, my lord?"

Cedric held up the mysterious note. "Where did this come from?"

The butler held his hands up in confusion. "I fear I do not know."

Cedric frowned. He had presumed that Winters had placed the note in the library. Certainly none of the other servants would have entered his private sanctuary. Not in his current mood anyway. In the past two weeks they had all made a concerted effort to avoid him.

So where the devil had it come from?

For a brief moment he considered consigning the letter to the fire. Certainly no respectable individual would slip into his library and leave such an odd message.

Then he paused as he realized that it might have been left by a tenant who was too proud to be seen begging on the doorsteps of Hartshore Park.

If that were the case, then he had to make an appearance.

Damn. He pulled out his pocket watch to discover it was a quarter to five.

He would have to hurry if he was to make it on time.

"Have Greenly saddle Firefly. I shall meet him at the door in ten minutes."

"At once, my lord."

Going in search of his greatcoat and hat, Cedric paused long enough to slip a loaded pistol into his pocket. He did not believe that anyone would set such a ridiculous plot to harm him, but he was not going to take foolish risks.

A quarter of an hour later he had entered the center of the woods with no sight yet of the mysterious letter-writer.

Gads, he sighed in annoyance. Surely he was not on yet another fool's errand?

Coming around a bend in the path, Cedric abruptly realized he was at the spot where he had first encountered Emma lodged in the mud. He unconsciously brought Firefly to a halt, a savage pain ripping through his body.

Even now he had only to close his eyes to smell her scent, to see her ridiculous gray gown and shadowed emerald eyes. . . .

"Hello, Cedric."

He blinked as a vision conjured by his fevered brain stepped from behind a tree. Good Lord, was he becoming unhinged?

Then a sudden breeze rippled through the opening and the black cape swirled close to her frame.

No. No vision, he acknowledged in disbelief, slowly dismounting. It was Emma, standing precisely where he had first seen her.

"Emma." He gave a shake of his head, attempting to gather his stunned wits. "You are the one who left the note?"

She slowly moved forward. "Yes."

"What is it? Your father? Has he been captured?"

"He is well and in London," she swiftly reassured him.

His brows drew together as he studied her pale face.

He could not deny a fierce flood of pleasure at seeing her. Or the tempting urge to pull her into his arms. It had been far, far too long since he had seen her. But the memory that it had been her own choice to leave Kent brought him up short.

"What are you doing here?"

Her tongue peeked out to wet her lips, as if the sight of his set features made her uneasy.

"You said that you loved me."

He flinched at her soft words. "Yes, after which you promptly fled," he harshly reminded her.

The emerald eyes seemed to darken. "I was frightened."

"Of me?"

"Never," she denied, taking another step closer. Close enough that he could smell the warm scent of her skin. He clenched his hands at his sides. "I was afraid of myself."

"Why?"

It took a long while before she met his gaze squarely. "I was in London when my father was arrested and his true identity became known. It was . . . horrid," she confessed in uneven tones. "I could not walk out the door without my supposed friends turning away in disgust or having their laughter following behind me. I simply wished to disappear."

"So you came to Kent," he finished, battling his instinctive surge of sympathy. On the last occasion his sympathy had led to a battered heart.

"Yes."

"You have not told me why you are here."

She lifted her hands in a helpless motion. "Because I love you."

He sucked in a sharp breath, his eyes narrowing at her unexpected declaration.

Love?

Women in love did not bolt in terror rather than accept a gentleman's proposal.

"And?"

She blinked at his clipped tone. "And I wish to be with you."

"Rather an abrupt change of heart, isn't it, my dear?" he forced himself to mutter.

"Cedric," she whispered in shock.

It was more difficult than he would ever believe to not simply accept her words and carry her back to Hartshore Park. How many nights had he dreamed of just this moment? How many mornings had he awoken expecting to find her in his bed?

But he could not risk his heart until he was certain she would not simply disappear once again.

"Do you know that I arose at the break of dawn the morning after the Valentine ball and rushed to Mayford with every intention of asking you to be my wife?" he demanded as he shoved his hands into the pockets of his coat. "I spent the entire night rehearsing precisely how I would say the words, how I would convince you that I would take care of you, how I would devote my life to making you happy. Imagine how foolish I felt to discover that you had bolted rather than face my proposal."

A dark flush of regret stained her countenance. "I am sorry, Cedric."

"I even packed my bags to follow you, when I realized that I could not chase you forever. I am not Apollo."

She reached out to place a tentative hand upon his arm. "And I am not Daphne," she insisted. "I have no desire to run from you, Cedric."

His gaze lowered to her hand. "What if I say it is too late?"

There was a moment of bleak silence before she answered. "Then I will go to Cassie and ask if she still wishes to have me as a companion. I am not leaving Kent."

His gaze snapped upward to probe the depths of her clear emerald eyes.

"Even when everyone knows who you are?" he demanded roughly.

"The only one who matters is you. It has taken me too long to realize that."

His breath caught in his throat at the love shimmering openly in her beautiful eyes. The shadows that had haunted her for so long were gone.

With great care he lifted his hand to cup her cheek. "You are not going to disappear into the mist?"

With a brilliant smile she lifted her arms and firmly circled his neck. The feel of her soft form pressed close to his own made all his lingering doubts vanish. The barriers had been well and truly lowered.

"Like it or not, you are irrevocably stuck with me, my lord."

"Emma." He buried his head in the curve of her neck, inhaling the fresh scent of her. "I thought I had lost you forever."

Somehow she managed to snuggle even closer, making a molten heat flow through his blood.

"I have been an utter fool," she whispered. "I love you, Cedric."

He turned his head so that he could trail his lips over her satin skin to at last brush her mouth.

"And I adore you, Emma Cresswell," he murmured, thoroughly enjoying her shivers of delight beneath his caress.

Then with a smooth motion he dropped to one knee and claimed her hand.

"What are you doing?" she exclaimed in surprise.

"I will not have my hours of rehearsal wasted," he informed her with a warm smile. "Emma, I promise to care for you, to love you, and give you all the security you desire. Will you marry me?"

Quite unexpectedly she lowered herself to her own knees, framing his face with her hands.

"On one condition."

Decidedly distracted by the intimacy of their position and the knowledge that they were very much alone, Cedric was ready to promise any condition.

"Oh?"

"That you will always surprise me," she said simply.

Cedric tilted back his head to laugh with sheer joy. "That I believe can easily be arranged," he assured her, reaching beneath his jacket to remove a slip of paper he had kept close to his heart since the night of the Valentine ball. He firmly pressed it into her hand.

Clearly curious, she glanced at her name scrolled onto the paper.

"What is this?"

"The Valentine that you pinned to my sleeve."

Her eyes widened. "You drew my name?"

"It was fate," he said as his arms reached out to encircle her waist and draw her close. Then with a smooth motion he lay back until he was stretched upon the hard ground with her delicious body atop him. Precisely as they had been during that first magical kiss. "From the moment I found you stuck in the mud. And now I intend to do precisely what I wanted to do then."

Unlike that first time, Emma did not struggle, but instead settled herself more comfortably as she smiled into his dark countenance.

"Why, Lord Hartshore, this is hardly proper," she teased.

His hand cupped the back of her neck as he began to bring her mouth within kissing distance.

"Well, I have never been a particularly proper sort of chap," he warned her.

She readily brushed his lips with her own, her hands moving to tangle in his hair.

"Thank goodness."

ABOUT THE AUTHOR

Debbie Raleigh lives with her family in Missouri. She is currently working on *The Wedding Wish* (Rachel's story) coming in April 2002. Debbie loves to hear from readers, and you may write to her c/o Zebra Books. Please include a self-addressed stamped envelope if you wish a response.

More Zebra Regency Romances

DO YOU HAVE THE
HOHL COLLECTION?

The Queen of
Romance

Cassie Edwards